The Midr

Michel Tournier was born in 1924, trained as a philosopher, became an expert on Germany and the German language, and spent some years working in French radio, television and book publishing before devoting himself full time to writing. Tournier was described by the *Observer* as 'the most gifted and original novelist to emerge in France since the war'. His first novel, *Friday or the Other Island*, won the Grand Prix du Roman of the Académie Française in 1967; his second, *The Erl King*, won the Prix Goncourt in 1970. All his five novels have been translated into English, together with a volume of short stories, *The Fetishist*, and an autobiographical volume, *The Wind Spirit*.

*Also by Michel Tournier
and available in Minerva*

Gilles and Jeanne
Gemini
The Fetishist
The Four Wise Men

MICHEL TOURNIER

The Midnight Love Feast

Translated from the French by Barbara Wright

Minerva

A Minerva Paperback
THE MIDNIGHT LOVE FEAST

First published in Great Britain 1991
by William Collins Sons & Co. Ltd
This Minerva edition published 1992
by Mandarin Paperbacks
Michelin House, 81 Fulham Road, London SW3 6RB

Minerva is an imprint of the Octopus Publishing Group,
a division of Reed International Books Ltd

First published in France under the title *Le Médianoche
Amoureux* by Editions Gallimard 1989

Copyright © Editions Gallimard 1989
Translation copyright © Barbara Wright 1991

A CIP catalogue record for this title
is available from the British Library
ISBN 0 7493 9940 6

Printed and bound in Great Britain
by Cox & Wyman Ltd, Reading, Berks

This book is sold subject to the condition
that it shall not, by way of trade or otherwise,
be lent, resold, hired out, or otherwise circulated
without the publisher's prior consent in any form
of binding or cover other than that in which
it is published and without a similar condition
including this condition being imposed
on the subsequent purchaser.

The Taciturn Lovers

HE: Yves Oudalle. That's my name. Born in Yport on 21 March 1930 – father a fisherman and mother from a large family. My father fished inshore from a smack he could have handled on his own but which he operated with a mate until my older brother was of an age to help him. It was the presence of this brother that determined my life. I was jealous of him, and had an obsessive need to outdo him. The solution lay before my eyes every time the big Wednesday market took us to Fécamp, the port of the Newfoundland fishing-boats. My brother fished for mackerel, herring and scallops; I would fish for cod. He left every morning and came back in the evening on a seven-metre boat; I would embark for four months on one of the seventy-metre long, eleven-metre wide trawlers that I admired in the winter when they were in dry dock being refitted in preparation for the great departure. He belonged to *le petit métier* – inshore fishing; but I would belong to *le grand métier* – deep-sea fishing. I would go to the Banks of Newfoundland and the Arctic, in the coldest waters in the world, with a fifty-man crew. I had only one desire: to leave school and board ship. The law did not allow ship's boys to be taken on until they were fifteen. But I knew you could leave before that age if you were under the guardianship of a relative. And so a distant uncle, a ship's captain, gave me the opportunity to sign my first contract at the age of thirteen.

I don't know what life was like for children in factories, down coal mines, or isolated in the plains of the Beauce among flocks of sheep. But for a ship's boy on a deep-sea fishing boat, it was hell. As the Larousse dictionary of the time coolly wrote at the entry for 'scapegoat': 'the ship's boy was the crew's scapegoat'. He was exploited, trampled underfoot, beaten and sodomized, and for this the men had two justifications: 'We all went through it. He'll be treated like the rest', and 'It's all part of the job.' The job also consisted of gutting the cod, emptying it of its blood and washing it in a big bucket, then throwing it down into the hold. This meant that a ship's boy had to keep his hands in sea water for the sixteen to twenty hours that the fishing 'day' lasts, and it's easy to imagine the frightful stumps his hands became: purple, chapped, cracked, eaten into by the brine; hands that no longer looked human. I still bear the stigmata of this terrible apprenticeship.

But the work was not the worst part. Because the 'dogsbody', the lowest of the low in the ship's hierarchy, must be at the beck and call of the crew who are often drunk with fatigue, nervous tension and alcohol. He normally assists the cook, running from one deck to another with soup tureens, coffee-pots and mess-tins, or he passes round twenty lighted cigarettes which fill his mouth and asphyxiate him. And it is not a rare event for his brief sleep to be interrupted by a few rough kicks that force him out of his palliasse to serve the night watch. And how could I complain? Hadn't I gone to all possible lengths to get myself there! 'You asked for it, you half-wit!' And on top of all this, there was the strange, overwhelming solidarity of the crew who, without the slightest political indoctrination, knew only too well that, as a body, they were the victims of an economic and social system. The same applies to every exploited class. Poverty and suffering make members of those classes savage in their dealings with one another, but they all know that this poverty and suffering must be attributed to the machine and its masters. For the Newfoundland fisherman, the master is the shipowner. And the ordinary Newfoundland fisherman never sees him; he is a mythical bloodsucker, a hidden ogre. It is only the captain who comes face to face with him after the catch. The captain gives him a verbal report, a mixture of figures and human details, and from the start he takes it for granted that a serious injury or even a death on board will be less upsetting to the shipowner than an unprofitable trip. The re-engagement of the whole crew, and his own, depend on this interview.

6

I didn't meet my shipowner until I had myself become a captain. But I was sixteen when his two children made an appearance on the *Frehel*, a stern trawler which had been exploring the Greenland banks for a week without much success. The atmosphere on board was stormy, and the arrival of that boy of eighteen and that little girl of ten, the shipowner's own flesh and blood, couldn't have come at a worse time. Nevertheless, ever since a launch had brought them from a luxury yacht, the captain had been making every effort to do them the honours of the *Frehel* and to initiate them into *le grand métier*. I was too taken up with my duties to have time to observe the progress of the forty-eight hours they spent on board, but I was the quite unintentional agent of a mishap which must certainly have added spice to their experience. I was sweeping the after deck when the first mate suddenly appeared with our two visitors. He was a slow-witted colossus who took inordinate pride in both an extremely well-kept black beard and the expensive cigars he never stopped sucking on. He stopped by me and pointed to his cigar, which had gone out. Hampered by my broom, I pulled out of my pocket the big copper paraffin-lighter that was the mark of one of my duties as ship's boy, and sent a long, smoky flame spurting out of it. As ill luck would have it, the moment I held it up to the first mate's cigar, the boat heaved and made me topple forward. The sputtering flame plunged into that beautiful, glossy, gleaming beard. The man leapt back with a roar. There was a herring barrel within his reach, on top of which lay a big cod. He grabbed it by the tail and slapped my face with it as hard as he could. This was what is called a 'bank whip' on the trawlers, a slimy barbed drubbing that every ship's boy has experienced. I was too much inured to ill-treatment to be unduly affected by this particular blow. But the shipowner's young son apparently took it less well. 'Come on, Nadège,' he said, turning on his heel with his sister. I watched them walk away, thinking that their disapproval would only make my offence more heinous in the eyes of the first mate. But at least I had learnt the name of the little girl.

SHE: It's true that my name is Nadège. My father used to say: 'I chose that name for her to oblige her to be beautiful. If she isn't, it will make her look ridiculous.' Well, I have always suffered from this name as if I had indeed been ridiculed, because I am the very opposite of beautiful. There is a crucial moment in the life of a little girl, a decisive ordeal after which nothing is as it was before. Watch them jostle at the school gate. It takes no more than a glance to recognize the innocent ones, the ones who have not yet undergone the ordeal. They may be skinny or plump, graceful or gauche, radiant or melancholy, but it is obvious that it doesn't bother them, they aren't even aware of it. The others, the ones who have been through the ordeal, the initiates, recognize themselves in the mirror they carry deep in their hearts. One accursed day, these girls have asked themselves the question (fateful, yet so absurd): 'Am I pretty?' What happens at that moment is that the whole alienation of the feminine condition falls on their shoulders. Yes, women ought to militate to be granted, as men are, the right to be ugly. There should also be an end to that deplorable convention according to which no one must ever ask a woman over thirty how old she is, must even avoid any reference to her age, as if it was somehow a shameful disease. To behave in this way is to identify oneself with the current view that once a woman has become adult, and has therefore stopped being a fresh, desirable prey, she is only good to be thrown on the scrap-heap.

Am I pretty? I didn't put that question to my mirror, but to my mother. I was eleven. She dazzled me by her beauty, her elegance, her fashionable sophistication. We had just come from the oculist, who had placed a big pair of horn-rimmed spectacles on my tiny little nose. You will agree that the question could no longer be avoided. I squinted into all the shop windows along the street to try to catch my reflection. It would have been normal for me to ask: 'Do these glasses suit me?' But the 'crucial question' somehow took advantage of its resemblance to that innocuous question to insinuate itself in its place. 'Am I pretty?' I can still hear my mother's reply. It has tattooed itself on my skin for all time: 'No, but you look nice, and intelligent, and that's much better.' I was in despair. Because niceness and intelligence didn't mean a thing to me. There was only one alternative: pretty or miserable. With this simple remark, my mother had just doomed me to misery. 'That's much better.' How could I have believed that assertion, tossed off with such gay abandon, when my mother herself seemed to have made every effort to prove to other people, and no doubt also to herself, that even though she had been born in Fécamp into a family that had lived in the Pays de Caux for several generations, she was nevertheless one of the most brilliant women in the world of international shipping?

Nice and intelligent, instead of pretty and elegant. It took me years to come to terms with this fate. I finally conceded that even though it wasn't 'much better', on the other hand it wasn't necessarily a malediction. Although these two qualities sometimes seemed to be mutually exclusive. Is it a sign of intelligence that I am acutely aware of stupidity, and have an infallible flair for detecting it? With men in whom I have spotted it, I veer between immediate, radical and implacable rejection, and amused indulgence, contempt tinged with pity. 'For goodness' sake, be handsome, but keep your mouth shut!' With this request I have caused more than one man to turn tail.

As my intelligent appearance and glasses suggested, I went to university and got a degree in classics at Rouen. That was where I met Alexis, who was studying to become a professor of philosophy. Philosophers are professionals of the intellect. What other people cultivate as amateurs – wit, subtlety, acuity, penetration, intuition, synthetic vision – they make a profession of. That was how he got me. Not many girls, I imagine, have been seduced by a critical reading of pages of Leibnitz, Kant, Hegel and Heidegger. That was what happened to me. With hindsight, I see it as ridiculous, but I'm not ashamed of it. We married. Much too young, in the unanimous opinion of our families. The upheavals of May 1968 brought us together and then separated us. It's difficult for a couple to survive such an experience. I never stopped mocking Alexis's revolutionary fervour. It's true that he had always seen his role as professor of philosophy in the Socratic sense – as that of an awakener, an agitator, a sublime troublemaker. He greeted May 1968 as a personal Advent. I saw things differently. In actual fact, for him everything was resolved by talk, an irrepressible verbal flow that swept everything aside – obstacles, opponents, and simple common sense. He confused taking power with taking the floor, and I didn't fail to point this out to him.

Covered in ridicule, I withdrew to the bosom of my family in Fécamp. The men of the Pays de Caux have a reputation for taciturnity, and that was the quality I most appreciated after the verbosity unleashed by the events of 1968. I decided to turn over a new leaf, to put myself on a diet of dry bread – but even so, not of water, because I didn't give up the habit I had got into in the Latin Quarter of spending hours in cafés. Respectable Fécamp society was shocked to see me hanging around in the bistrots in town and down at the port. That was where I met Oudalle. He was hiring a crew for a boat he had just been given command of by the *Sécherie*, as the deep-sea fishing company was familiarly called. He was sitting at a table at the back of the café; the applicants came and sat down with him, one after the other, with their papers, the way people go to confession. Sturdy, slow, with a blue gaze under his blond eyebrows, Oudalle seemed to be as talkative as a polar bear. I fell in love with him on the spot. He reminded me later that this was not our first meeting. Twenty years before, during a family cruise on a yacht belonging to the Company, my father had sent my brother and me to spend a couple of days on one of our fleet's trawlers which was working nearby. This was part of our education. From the start I was revolted by the atmosphere of brutal melancholy that reigned on this floating penal colony. I actually saw one violent scene: the first mate picked up a codfish and used it to slap a young ship's boy who had nearly burnt the man's face while lighting his cigar. I should certainly not have recognized that adolescent in the polar bear in the café, but he had heard my Christian name – one rare enough for him not to have forgotten it in circumstances which in themselves were fairly striking.

I have had occasion to discuss with him the necessarily hostile feelings that the men who work at sea harbour against the shipowners, whom they see as bloodsuckers. But we – the children of the Ogre – had been brought up to hero-worship the men of *le grand métier*, those Iceland fishermen extolled by a host of writers from Victor Hugo to Roger Vercel, by way of Pierre Loti and Joseph Conrad. This was our family epic, our own world, grandiose and sombre, with its heroes and its villains, and above all the fleet of sailing-boats, and then steam boats, and now diesel-powered vessels that the Company had commissioned in almost a century's existence, scrupulously exact models of which filled the glass cases in the *Sécherie*'s main office. Naturally, all this played some part in my feelings for Oudalle. He went to sea three weeks after our first meeting, and for the next five years I found it exciting to wait for him, to think about him, to write to him, although there was another me who sneered at this role of the fisherman's wife, and potential widow, roaming the desolate beaches in her dark veils, which I enjoyed playing. Why should I deny it? Literature obsessed me – it still does – and I couldn't help being moved when I thought about Gaud, in Pierre Loti's novel, who wastes away with lonely love while her Yann is sailing the cold seas. One passage in particular disturbed me by a hint of fetishism surprising in so naïve a book: *Very often she used to touch Yann's belongings, his beautiful wedding-clothes, unfolding them, folding them up again like a maniac – and especially one of his blue woollen jerseys that had retained the shape of his body; when you threw it gently on to the table, of its own accord and as if from habit, it delineated the contours of his shoulders and his chest.*

HE: My uncle used to say that a Newfoundland fisherman ought not to marry. Obviously, there is the fate of the wife, a grass-widow for three-quarters of the year, left alone at home with the children. To try to prevent their father from becoming a stranger to them, she talks about him as much as she can. But what can she tell them over the years, unless she possesses the imagination of a novelist? Nor must she make the missing man out to be a saint, a hero, a good genie. Because there is the ordeal of his return, the difficulty of his reintegration into an environment that has learnt to live without him. Everybody round the table grows tired of his stories of ice floes, storms and fish, and for his part he is no longer in touch with the everyday life of the neighbourhood. How often does everyone long for the father to leave on his next voyage!

I have to admit that it's in conversation that the difficulty, for a seaman, of living as a couple becomes apparent. Through constant separation, you end up having nothing to say to each other.

My case was complicated by a social, or at least a professional, dimension. In the eyes of his fellows, a seaman who marries the boss's daughter is a turncoat, almost a traitor. All the more so in that he is suspected of succumbing to the lure of money. Deep-sea crews rarely come from Fécamp. Fécamp is the big town, the domain of the shipowners. The men come from the small towns and villages in the Pays de Caux. They belong to the same underprivileged classes as the agricultural labourers. As I was born in Yport (1,000 inhabitants), I almost count as a bourgeois. Well, I married a young lady from the big town – rich, into the bargain, and educated. Divorced, it's true, but from a professor of philosophy. That would have been enough to intimidate me if I had been in my first youth. But *le grand métier* had kept me a bachelor for a long time, and it was only after I had got my captain's ticket at the training college in Fécamp that I began to think of getting married. No doubt I wanted to become presentable in the eyes of my new family and to have at least an officer's cap to show my fiancée. Yet another concession to the rich. But all those years spent in the all-male society of a crew is no preparation for conjugal life. In the beginning I could draw on a certain mythological capital in Nadège's mind. She had been brought up in the bosom of that dynasty of shipowners to revere deep-sea fishing. She listened passionately when I spoke of my voyages. And then the capital ran out. Her passion turned into respect. And after that, all she could offer me was patience. And patience has its limits . . .

SHE: And yet it's true that we come from the same background – it's clear from our conversations. Don't you remember? One day you dared to make me a declaration that would have sounded extraordinary to any other woman. I was naked, standing in front of you. You ran your hands over my body, slowly and with wonder. You said:

HE: You are as beautiful as a cod!

SHE: I was delighted, by virtue of the freemasonry to which we both belong, of which that word is the sign.

HE: Cod, Bank cod, haddock, hake, whiting, ling, pollack, stockfish . . . We have as many words for this fetish-fish as the Arab has for the camel. And it is true that our cod is beautiful, with its three dorsal fins, its two anal fins, its mottled skin with its leopard's spots, and above all . . .

SHE: . . . above all the little beard under its chin which embodies its sensitivity and humour.

HE: After all, a hunter is allowed to call his wife my duck or my chick. And then, anyway . . . Undine, Melusina, the Mermaids. The woman-fish has her own legend, her own magic.

Unfortunately, something happened that upset our free-masonry, and at the same time my private life. I had put into port at St-Pierre-et-Miquelon when on 23 March 1973 I received a laconic and peremptory telegram:

Ship permanently decommissioned conclusion voyage. This information not to be communicated crew. Signed: Cod.

13

Even though I had been expecting this sudden end to Fécamp as the capital of cod-fishing, this was a bitter blow. But how could the old Fécamp shipowning families be blamed for giving up after a ruinous struggle against the march of time? Salt cod, food for the poor produced by the poor, was being replaced by frozen or deep-frozen cod at a time when the banks, depleted by over-fishing, were becoming rare. Most of the *grand métier* trawlers were being sent to the scrap-yard. And I came ashore and found myself out of work at the age of forty-three. So there I was, a total landlubber and a full-time husband. What an upheaval!

It took me a long time to realize that the decision you then reached was painful for you, and that it was for my sake, to save me and to save our marriage. Six months after I came back for good you closed our beautiful flat whose windows looked out on to the port of Fécamp, and we moved to Grouin-du-Sud, near Avranches, to a house your family had used as a summer residence and which you had had refurbished to make it habitable all year round. This migration from one end of Normandy to the other had a very precise purpose: to remove me from Fécamp society, where the crisis and decay of my profession had fostered a horrible atmosphere; and above all to give back to me in a new form the sea of which I had been deprived by the end of my career.

In a new form, yes, but that's putting it mildly! Because the Pays de Caux doesn't recognize the word beach, with all its connotations of soft sands and hordes of summer visitors. Tall chalk cliffs, permanently assaulted by the waves and the elements which tear rocky strips from them, shores covered in pebbles which get churned up by the undertow and come crashing down like thunder – that is the nature of our entire coastline. I am not ashamed to admit that I can't swim, even though I have spent years at sea. Bathing, sunbathing, and other summer frolics, as well as the bric-à-brac of so-called underwater fishing with its masks, flippers, wetsuits, guns and oxygen bottles – all that is for Parisians, for rich idlers who come to play with the ocean for a few days. We seamen don't know how to play with the ocean.

At Grouin I discovered the opposite of the sea, the reverse of the ocean: low tide, and the way it's used, fishing on foot for shellfish. A kind of fishing for the native population, unknown to holiday-makers, for which one wears tightly laced espadrilles and a female tramp's clothes and headgear, and which demands a close relationship with the foreshore, that ambiguous, contentious, magical zone, alternately covered and uncovered by the rise and fall in the level of the sea.

The low-water fisherman lives according to the rhythm of the tides. The times of the flood and ebb tides are more important to him than those of the rising and setting of the sun. He obeys the great mysterious astronomical clock whose numerals are called solstices, equinoxes, spring-tides, syzygies. On his bedside table, the official tide-table determines months in advance the day when he should plan a picnic on the shore, get up at three in the morning, or even give up altogether because it's the time of the neap tides.

After my beautiful modern trawler, a ship of 1,485 tons, had been sent to the breaker's yard, I dressed up as a vagrant and went to sea with a bucket, salt-box, spade, sack, pronged harpoon, basket and shrimping-net, not forgetting a bottle to bring back some sea-water to cook the shrimps in, but above all with the anticipated joy of long hours spent roaming the beds of water plants, the mud flats, pools, rocks, lagoons and quicksands. In the evenings I would tip on to the kitchen table sea urchins and mussels, octopuses and velvet swimming crabs, razor clams and limpets and, if the sea gods had blessed us, a lobster with heavy blue claws and a fearsome caudal whiplash.

SHE: In the beginning I thought I ought to come with you on those excursions, and no doubt you for your part honestly tried to let me share the pleasure you found in foreshore fishing. But we soon had to admit that it was a solitary pleasure, an egotistical joy that is ruined if you try to share it. Your efforts to get me to be ready at the time determined by the terrible official tide-table, to teach me to extract the razor clam – *solen ensis*, you would specify with the pedantry of the autodidact – from its bed of sand, using a rigid steel wire with a conical sinker on its end, and to steel myself at last to plunge my naked hand under the mane of seaweed covering a rock and grab hold of the powerful, ice-cold body of an octopus or conger eel, and . . . and . . . and . . . I don't remember what else, because all the advice and rebukes you never stopped raining down on my head left so few traces – yes, on the whole, that fruitless apprenticeship served more to divide us than to bring us together. And to crown it all, there was our extraordinary meeting with Patricio Lagos, whose inventions took on a symbolic meaning for us.

HE: It was a bright September morning after an equinoctial tide which had given the bay a devastated, frantic, almost pathetic air. We were walking along a shore sparkling with mirrors of water which made the flatfish quiver; a shore strewn with unusual shell-fish – whelks, cockles, ormers, clams. But we weren't in the mood for fishing, and spent most of our time looking over towards the south coast, which was shrouded in a milky fog. Yes, there was mystery in the air, almost tragedy, and I wasn't particularly surprised when you drew my attention to two human bodies clasped in each other's arms and covered in sand, about a hundred metres away. We immediately ran up to what we took to be drowned corpses. But they weren't drowned corpses covered in sand. They were two statues sculpted in sand, of strange and poignant beauty. The bodies were curled up in a slight depression, and encircled by a strip of grey, mud-stained cloth, which added to their realism. One thought of Adam and Eve, before God came and breathed the breath of life into their nostrils of clay. One also thought of the inhabitants of Pompeii whose bodies were fossilized under the hail of volcanic ash from Vesuvius. Or of the men of Hiroshima, vitrified by the explosion of the Atom Bomb. Their tawny faces, spangled with flakes of mica, were turned towards each other and separated by an impassable distance. Only their hands and legs were touching.

We stood for a moment in front of these recumbent figures, as if at the edge of a newly-opened grave. At this moment a strange sort of devil suddenly emerged from some invisible hole, barefoot and stripped to the waist, wearing frayed jeans. He began a graceful dance, making sweeping arm movements which seemed to be greeting us, and then to be bowing to the recumbent figures as a preliminary to picking them up and raising them to the heavens. The deserted, slack-water shore, the pale light, this couple made of sand, this dancing madman – all of these things surrounded us with a melancholy, unreal phantasmagoria. And then the dancer came to a standstill, as if suddenly in a trance. After which he bowed, knelt, prostrated himself before us, or rather – as we realized – before an apparition that had loomed up behind us. We turned round. To the right, the Tomberlaine rock was emerging from the haze. But most impressive, suspended like a Saharan mirage above the clouds, was the pyramid of the abbey of Mont Saint Michel, with all its glistening pink roof-tiles and glinting stained-glass windows.

Time had stopped. Something had to happen to restart it. It was a few drops of water tickling my feet that did it. A foam-capped tongue licked my toes. Listening carefully, we could hear the incessant rustling of the sea that was stealthily creeping up on us. In less than an hour this immense area, now laid bare to the wind and sun, would be returned to the glaucous, merciful depths.

'But they'll be destroyed!' you exclaimed.

With a sad smile the dancer bowed, as a sign of approval. Then he sprang up and mimed the return of the tide, as if he wanted to accompany it, encourage it, even provoke it by his dance. African sorcerers do much the same when they want to induce rain or drive out demons. And the sea obeyed, first flowing round the edges of the depression in which the couple were lying, then finding a breach that allowed through an innocent trickle of water, then two, then three. The joined hands were the first affected and they disintegrated, leaving in suspense stumps of amputated wrists. Horrified, we watched the capricious and inexorable dissolution of this couple which we persisted in feeling to be human, close to us, perhaps premonitory. A stronger wave broke over the woman's head, carrying away half her face, then it was the man's right shoulder that collapsed, and we thought them even more touching in their mutilation.

A few minutes later we were obliged to beat a retreat and abandon the sand basin with its swirling, frothy eddies. The dancer came with us, and we discovered that he was neither mad nor dumb. His name was Patricio Lagos and he came from Chile, more precisely from Chiloe Island, where he was born, which is off the south coast of Chile. It is inhabited by Indians adept in exploiting the forests. He had studied dancing and sculpture at the same time, in Santiago, and had then emigrated to the Antipodes. He was obsessed by the problem of time. Dance, the art of the moment, ephemeral by nature, leaves no trace and suffers from its inability to become rooted in any kind of continuity. Sculpture, the art of eternity, defies time by seeking out indestructible materials. But in so doing, what it finally finds is death, for marble has an obvious funerary vocation. On the Channel and Atlantic coasts, Lagos had discovered the phenomenon of tides governed by the laws of astronomy. Now the tide gives a rhythm to the shore dancer's games, and at the same time suggests the practice of ephemeral sculpture.

'My sand sculptures live,' he declared, 'and the proof of this is that they die. It's the opposite of the statuary in cemeteries, which is eternal because it is lifeless.'

And so he feverishly sculpted couples in the wet sand just uncovered by the ebbing tide, and both his dancing and his sculpture stemmed from the same inspiration. It was important that his work should be finished at the very moment of slackwater, for this must be a parenthesis of rest and meditation. But the great moment was the return of the tide and the terrible ceremony of the destruction of the work. A slow, meticulous, inexorable destruction, governed by an astronomical destiny, and which should be encircled by a sombre, lyrical dance. 'I celebrate the pathetic fragility of life,' he said. That was when you asked him a question of prime importance to us, which he answered in what I considered an obscure, mysterious way.

SHE: Yes, I raised the question of silence. Because according to our customs, dance is accompanied by music, and in one way it is only music embodied, music made flesh. So there was something paradoxical and strange about the dance he was performing in silence round his recumbent sand-figures. But he unreservedly rejected the word silence. 'Silence?' he said, 'but there *is* no silence! Nature detests silence, as she abhors a vacuum. Listen to the shore at low tide: it babbles through the thousands of moist lips it half-opens to the skies. *Volubile*. When I was learning French, I fell in love with that graceful, ambiguous word. It is another name for bindweed, whose fragile, interminable stem twines round the sturdier plants it comes across, and it finally chokes them under its disordered profusion studded with white trumpets. The rising tide too is voluble. It entwines the chests and thighs of my clay lovers with its liquid tentacles. And it destroys them. It is the kiss of death. But the rising tide is also voluble in the childish babble it whispers as it flows over the ooze. It insinuates its salty tongues into the sands with moist sighs. It would like to speak. It is searching for its words. It's a baby burbling in its cradle.'

And he stayed behind and left us, with a little farewell wave and a sad smile, when we reached the beach.

HE: He's a bit mad, your sculptor-dancer, but it's true that by crossing Normandy from east to west, by emigrating from the pebbles of Fécamp to the sands of Mont Saint Michel, we changed ocean sounds. The waves on the shores of the Pays de Caux smash thousands of stones in a rocky pandemonium. Here, the tide murmurs as it advances with seagull's steps.

SHE: This false silence hasn't been good for you. In Fécamp I loved a taciturn man. You despised all the conventional chit-chat with which human relations surround themselves. Good-morning, good-evening, how are you, very well, and you? what filthy weather . . . You killed all that verbiage with a stern look. Here, you have become uncommunicative. There are grunts in your silences, grumbles in your asides.

HE: Just a moment! I never despised 'what filthy weather!' I don't think it's a waste of time to talk about the weather. It's an important subject to seamen. For me, weather reports are lyric poetry. But that's just it. The words we use ought to accord with the sky and the sea. The words appropriate to Fécamp don't correspond to the air in Avranches. Here there is something like a soft, insidious appeal, a demand that I don't know how to satisfy.

SHE: Here we are separated by an immense shore of silence, to which every day brings its low tide. The great logorrhoea of May 1968 made me dream of laconic wisdom, of words that were weighed, and rare, but full of meaning. We are sinking into an oppressive mutism that is just as empty as the student verbosity.

HE: Make up your mind! Nowadays you never stop reproaching me for my silence. No attack is too aggressive for you, no matter how hurtful it might be.

SHE: It's to get a rise out of you. I want a crisis, an explosion, a domestic scene. What is a domestic scene? It's the woman's triumph. It's when the woman has finally forced the man out of his silence by her nagging. Then he shouts, he rages, he's abusive, and the woman surrenders to being voluptuously steeped in this verbal downpour.

HE: Do you remember what they say about the Comte de Carhaix-Plouguer? When they're in company, his wife and he look as if they are the perfect couple. They exchange as many words as are necessary not to arouse curiosity. Though not one more, it's true. Because it's only a façade. Having discovered that his wife was unfaithful to him, the Count communicated his decision never again to talk to her when they were alone – and that was the last time he spoke to her. The extraordinary thing is that in spite of this silence, he managed to have three children with her.

SHE: I have never been unfaithful to you. But I would like to remind you that you sometimes don't even grant me the minimum of words necessary not to arouse people's curiosity. On Sundays, we usually lunch together in a restaurant on the coast. There are times when I am so ashamed of our silence that I move my lips soundlessly, to make the other customers think I'm talking to you.

HE: One morning, while we were having breakfast . . .

SHE: I remember. You were deep in your newspaper. You had disappeared behind the newspaper, which you were holding up like a screen. Could anyone be more boorish?

HE: You pressed the playback button on a little tape recorder you had just put down on the table. And then we heard a chorus of wheezing, rattling, gurgling, puffing and blowing and snoring, all of it orchestrated, rhythmic, returning to the point of departure with a reprise of the whole gamut. I asked you: 'What's that?' And you answered: 'It's you when you're asleep. That's all you have to say to me. So I record it.' 'I snore?' 'Obviously you snore! But you don't realize it. Now you can hear it. That's progress, isn't it?'

SHE: I didn't tell you everything. Incited by you, by your nocturnal snoring, I made enquiries. There is always an old student lying dormant in me. I discovered a science, rhonchology, a definition of nocturnal snoring. This is it: 'Respiratory sound during sleep, caused at the moment of inhalation by the vibration of the soft palate, due to the combined and simultaneous effect of the air entering through the nose and the air being drawn through the mouth.' There. I might add that this vibration of the soft palate is very similar to that of the sail of a boat when it's flapping in the wind. As you see, in both cases it's something to do with air.

HE: I appreciate this nautical aside, but I might remind you that I have never worked on a sailing boat.

SHE: As for the cures suggested by rhonchology, the most radical is tracheotomy; that's to say, opening an artificial orifice in the trachea so that breathing may be carried on outside the normal nasal passages. But there is also uvulo-palato-pharyngo-plastic-surgery – u.p.p.p.s. to initiates – which consists in resecting part of the soft palate including the uvula, so as to limit its vibratory potential.

HE: Young men ought to be told what they're letting themselves in for when they get married.

SHE: And vice versa! How could a girl ever suspect that the Prince Charming she loves makes a noise like a steam engine at night? Nevertheless, when she spends night after night by the side of a heavy snorer, she works out a rather bitter philosophy for herself.

HE: What does this rhonchological philosophy say?

SHE: That a couple is formed slowly over the years, and that with time the words they exchange take on increasing import-ance. At the beginning, deeds are enough. And then their dialogue becomes more extensive. It has to become deeper, too. Couples die from having no more to say to each other. My relations with a man are at an end on the evening when, coming back to him from a day spent elsewhere, I no longer want to tell him what I have done, or to hear him tell me how he has spent those hours away from me.

HE: It's true that I was never talkative. But it quite often happens that you interrupt one of my stories because it doesn't interest you.

SHE: Because you've already told it a hundred times.

HE: You made a diabolical suggestion on that subject one day, and I'm still wondering whether you were being serious. You suggested that I should number my stories. From then on, instead of telling you one from beginning to end with all the subtleties of the good story-teller, I should simply state its number, and you would understand at once. If I said 27, you would remember the story of my grandmother's dog which came aboard my trawler by mistake and returned to Fécamp a military hero. 71, and we would both have thought silently of the fidelity of those two gulls I saved and fed on one boat, and which knew how to find me on another vessel. 14, and my grandfather's odyssey during his one and only visit to Paris would have come to mind. So don't reproach me for my silence any more!

SHE: I know all your stories, and I even tell them better than you do. A good story-teller must be able to ring the changes.

HE: Not absolutely. Repetition is part of the game. There is a narrative ritual which children, for instance, respect. They are not concerned with novelty; they insist on the same story being told in the same words. The slightest change makes them leap up in indignation. In the same way, there is a ritual of daily life, of weeks, seasons, feast-days, years. A happy life is one that can cast itself in these moulds without feeling confined.

SHE: You're wrong to think that my idea of numbering your stories was only aimed at silencing you. I could just as well have used it to get you to talk. I would simply have said: 23. And you would straightaway have told me how you lived under siege in Le Havre from September 2nd to 13th, 1944. But I ask myself, honestly: would I have the heart to listen to the same story told indefinitely in the same words? Would I have the childlike imagination needed for that?

HE: I'm quite sure you would. You're lying, or you're lying to yourself. And there's the other point of view: mine. There's a certain, very dangerous concept which is quite likely to kill off the dialogue between a couple: the concept of the *innocent ear*. If a man changes his woman, he does so in order to find in the new woman an innocent ear for his stories. Don Juan was nothing but an incorrigible braggart, *un hâbleur* – a word of Spanish origin meaning a glib talker. A woman only interested him for the length of time – short, alas, and increasingly short – that she had faith in his *hâbleries*. If he detected the shadow of a doubt in her gaze, it cast a glacial chill over his heart and his genitals. And then he would leave, he would go off to look elsewhere for the exquisite, warm credulity that alone gave their true weight to his *hâbleries*. All this proves the importance of words in the life of a couple. And anyway, when one of the two sleeps with a third person, we say that he 'deceives' the other, which is to situate his betrayal in the domain of language. A man and a woman who never lied to each other and who immediately confessed all their betrayals would not be deceiving one another.

SHE: No doubt. But that would be a dialogue of cynics, and the wounds they inflicted on each other in the name of transparency would quite soon part them.

HE: Then people should lie?

SHE: Yes and no. Between the obscurity of lying and the transparency of cynicism, there is room for a whole range of light and shade in which the truth is known but not discussed, or else is deliberately ignored. In company, courtesy doesn't allow certain truths to be uttered bluntly. Why shouldn't there also be courtesy between couples? You're deceiving me, I'm deceiving you, but we

24

don't want to know about it. The only valid intimacy is of a twilight nature. 'Pull down the shade a little,' as the charming Paul Géraldy said.

HE: Between couples, perhaps, but certainly not between women. There, the crudest cynicism is calmly displayed. Ladies, amongst yourselves, you are appalling gossips! I was waiting at the hairdresser's one day, on the side marked 'Gentlemen', which was only separated from the ladies' salon by a half-partition. I was staggered by the complicity that united stylists, manicurists, shampoo girls and clients in a generalized babble in which the most intimate secrets of bodies and couples were laid bare without the slightest discretion.

SHE: And men in the company of other men keep such things to themselves, I suppose?

HE: More than you think. More than women do, in any case. Masculine vanity, which is generally so ridiculous, imposes a certain reticence on them in such matters. For instance, we aren't too fond of talking about our illnesses.

SHE: It's true that 'intimate secrets', as you so delicately put it, don't amount to much for men. Everything always comes down to figures, with them. So many times or so many centimetres. Women's secrets are far more subtle and obscure! As for our complicity, it's a complicity of the oppressed, and hence universal, because women are everywhere subjected to men's whims. No man will ever know the depth of the feeling of complicity that can unite two women, even when they are perfect strangers to each other. I remember a visit to Morocco. I was the only woman in our little group. As so often in the South, we were approached by a very young boy who spontaneously invited us to come to his house for tea. The father received us, surrounded by his sons – three or four of them, I don't remember exactly. The youngest one must just have learnt to walk. There was a blanket over a doorway which no doubt led to the bedrooms. Every so often it moved surreptitiously, and a black eye could be seen peeping through. The mother, the daughters, the grandmother, the mother-in-law, confined to the inner rooms, were waiting, listening, spying. I remember the way the women had protested when a running-water tap was installed in their houses. For them, that was the end of their trips to the village fountain, and of the long, delightful chats with the other women that these trips occasioned. When we left, I passed a girl on her way home. She smiled at me alone, because I was the only woman, and there was a world of warm fraternity in that smile. And when I say fraternity, I ought rather to say sorority, but the word doesn't exist in French.

HE: Perhaps because the thing itself is too rare to deserve a name.

SHE: It's principally because it's men who construct language. In a strange novel called *The Miracle of the Women's Island*, Gerhart Hauptmann invents his own version of the Robinson Crusoe story. He imagines that after a steamer has been shipwrecked, lifeboats exclusively occupied by women are cast up on a desert island. The result is a women's republic of about a hundred citizenesses.

HE: It must be hell!

SHE: Not at all. Quite the contrary! It's the great sorority. The idea Hauptmann champions is that if women fall out with one another, it's the fault of men. It is men who are the great sowers of discord among sisters, even among the sisterhood of nuns, whose shared confessor is a disruptive influence.

HE: Is that the miracle?

SHE: No. The miracle is that one day, after years of living in their happy sorority, one of the women discovers that she is inexplicably pregnant.

HE: The Holy Ghost, no doubt.

SHE: Everything might still be all right if she had given birth to a daughter. But the malignancy of fate saw to it that she had a son. The knell of the women's island had tolled. The virile virus was about to do its devastating work.

HE: In short, since you and I have the misfortune to belong to opposite sexes, since we have no more to say to each other, the only thing left for us to do is to separate. Let's at least do so with a flourish. We'll get all our friends together for a late-night dinner.

SHE: A *medianoche*, as the Spaniards call it.

HE: We'll choose the shortest night of the year so that our guests will leave as the sun is rising over the bay. We'll serve nothing but the produce of my foreshore fishing.

SHE: We'll talk to them, they'll talk to us, it will be a great palaver about the couple and love. Our *medianoche* will be a midnight love feast and a celebration of the sea. When all our guests have had their say, you will tap your knife on your glass and solemnly announce the sad news: 'Oudalle and Nadège are separating because they don't get on any more. Sometimes they even have words. Then a disagreeable silence surrounds them . . .' And when the last guest has gone, we'll put a notice on the front door: FOR SALE, and we too will go our different ways.

* * *

And so it was. Invitations were sent out for the summer solstice to all Nadège and Oudalle's friends. Nadège reserved all the rooms in the three hotels in Avranches. Oudalle, with two of his fishing friends, prepared a memorable banquet of foreshore fish.

It was still light when the first guests arrived. These were the ones who had had the farthest to travel, as they had come all the way from Arles. Then, almost immediately, their nearest neighbours rang the bell, and it was half an hour before the next influx arrived. More and more came, all through the night, in a constant balletic flow of cars, just as Nadège and Oudalle had wished, for they hadn't prepared a formal dinner round a table but a permanent buffet from which all the guests could help themselves no matter when they arrived. To start with, there was poached crab, a consommé of mussels with croûtons, and smoked eel. Then hermit-crabs flambéed in whisky, and smoke-dried sea urchins. In keeping with tradition, they waited for the twelfth stroke of midnight to serve the *plat de résistance* – lobster Pompadour garnished with sea cucumbers. Then the night continued with octopus with paprika, paellas of cuttlefish, and a fricassee of wrasse. With the first glimmers of dawn the guests were brought ormers in white wine, sea-anemone fritters, and scallops in champagne. Thus, it was a true marine *medianoche* with neither vegetables, fruit nor sugar.

A group of guests had gathered on the high terrace whose piles reached out onto the shore itself. Neither Nadège nor Oudalle could have said whose idea it was to tell the first story. That one was lost in the night, as no doubt were the second and the third. But surprised by what was taking place in their house, they saw to it that the subsequent narratives were recorded and preserved. There were thus nineteen, and these narratives were sometimes tales which began with the magical and traditional 'once upon a time', and sometimes short stories told in the first person, slices of life that were often raw and sordid. Nadège and Oudalle listened, astonished by these imaginary constructions they saw being built in their own house and which vanished as soon as the last word was uttered, giving way to other, equally ephemeral descriptions. They thought of Lagos's sand statues. They followed the slow work this succession of fictions was accomplishing in them. They had the feeling that the short stories – grimly realistic, pessimistic and demoralizing – were tending to further their separation and the break-up of their marriage, whereas on the contrary the tales – delectable, warm-hearted and tender – were working to bring them together. And while the short stories had at first commanded more attention by their weighty, melancholy truth, as the night wore on the tales gained in beauty and in strength, and finally reached the point of radiating an irresistible charm. In the first hours, Ange Crevet, the humiliated child full of hatred, Ernest the poacher, the suicidal Théobald, and Blandine's frightful father, and Lucie, the woman without a shadow, and a few others – all this grey, austere crowd exuded an atmosphere of morose hatred. But soon Angus, King Faust the Wise Man, Pierrot with his Columbine, Adam the dancer and Eve the perfumed lady, the Chinese painter and his Greek rival, formed the scintillating procession of a new, young and eternal wedding. And it was above all the last tale, the one about the two banquets, that rescued, so it seemed, daily conjugal life by elevating the actions repeated every day and every night to the level of a fervent, intimate ceremony.

The solstice sun was setting the silhouette of Mont Saint Michel aglow when the last guest stood up to take his leave after having told, to his hosts alone, the most beautiful tale no doubt ever invented. The incoming tide was flowing under the open-work floor of the terrace. The shellfish caressed by the waves opened their valves and let out the mouthful of water they had been retaining during the arid hours. The thousands upon thousands of parched throats on the foreshore filled themselves with the briny fluid and began to whisper. The shore was stammering in search of a language, as Lagos had understood so well.

'You didn't stand up, you didn't tap your glass with your knife, and you didn't announce the sad news of our separation to our friends,' said Nadège.

'Because the inevitability of our separation no longer seems so obvious to me since all those stories have entered my head,' Oudalle replied.

'What we lacked, in fact, was a house of words to live in together. In former times, religion provided couples with an edifice that was at the same time real – the church – and imaginary, peopled with saints, illuminated with legends, resounding with hymns, which protected them from themselves and from outside aggression. We lacked this edifice. Our friends have provided us with all the materials for it. Literature as a panacea for couples in distress . . .'

'We were like two carps buried in the mud of our daily life,' Oudalle concluded, ever true to his halieutic metaphors. 'From now on we shall be like two trout quivering side by side in the fast-flowing waters of a mountain stream.'

'Your seafood *medianoche* was exquisite,' Nadège added. 'I appoint you the head chef of my house. You shall be the high priest of my kitchens and the guardian of the culinary and manducatory rites that invest a meal with its spiritual dimension.'

All Saints' Day and the
Fairy-Ring Champignons

I was going to play in a polo match in Rio de Janeiro at the weekend. I was to join my wife, who had left four days earlier with my three best ponies. They would need at least that amount of time to recover from the fatigue and nervous exhaustion of a ten-hour flight. My wife would enjoy exercising them over the ground to relax them. As a horseman, obviously I owed it to myself to marry a horsewoman. It was the lack of this sort of complicity that had scuppered my two previous marriages.

I was temporarily a bachelor, then, and it may well have been this unusual circumstance (I am fundamentally and irremediably a conjugal man, *homo conjugalis*) that contributed to my making a pilgrimage back to my early youth. That evening, I was to fly from Roissy to Rio, with a stopover in Madrid. I told the servants they could have some time off, I shut up our house myself, and waited with my luggage for the taxi that was to take me to the airport. In my mind I had already left Paris, I was already in Rio with my wife and the friends from the equestrian club with whom we were going to stay, but above all with my dear nags, who would have recovered from the trauma of their flight.

My dreams were brutally shattered by the shock of reality – in the event, a notice hanging crookedly over the check-in desk for my flight: the said flight had been cancelled. Reason: a strike by the ground staff at Madrid Airport. I was dismayed. That was something that wouldn't have happened under Franco! Taking into account the times of the next flights and the time difference with Rio, my polo match was up the spout and I had made my beloved nags cross the Atlantic to no purpose. My wife would make the best of it: she adores flying, and my goodness, there's nothing tragic about a few days spent in the middle of the Brazilian spring.

On the other hand, this hitch had curiously cut me off from reality. The house was shut up, the staff dispersed, my ponies and my wife had flown. Absurdly kept in Paris, which I had to all intents and purposes left, I was floating in a strange, disturbing void. I felt that my life had in some way become 'exposed', like a loose tooth which only stays in its hole in the gum by force of habit. The slightest pressure of the tongue lays bare both its roots and the soft, bloodstained hole in the gum.

I took a taxi and stepped out on to my usual pavement, feeling at a loss through an excess of leisure. Carrying my suitcase in one hand and my cabin bag in the other, I pushed open the garden gate with my knee and walked up the drive. The damp November night had fallen, but the glaucous light from the street lamps illuminated the ground very clearly. I kicked back a pile of dead leaves, and in so doing uncovered a little cluster of mushrooms. 'It's just the right weather for fairy-ring champignons,' I thought.

There was a sinister atmosphere in the house. I'd gone, for God's sake, so what was I doing there? The refrigerator had nothing to offer me. The TV was blank. For a while I wandered round the deserted rooms which were too tidy not to make me feel like an intruder. I thought of going and having a bite at the little restaurant in the rue Le Sueur which stays open until midnight, but then the prospect revolted me. In the end, I undressed and went to bed.

'Just the right weather for autumn fairy-ring champignons.' Yes, because while the fairy-ring variety is mainly a spring mushroom, it has an autumn version which is darker, more compact, but no less tasty. I thought of the stunted mushrooms I had just seen. I thought of my childhood. During the war I was eight, nine, ten, eleven, twelve. We lived in the presbytery of a village in Burgundy. As best we could – but we could hardly complain in those miserable times. I used to scour the countryside on my bicycle, trying to glean something to eat from the peasants. I am not likely to forget the terrible weight of a trailer attached to a saddle post, or the bumpy strips of cork that very soon replaced rubber tyres. I went to the local primary school, where I was resented for my bourgeois origins, which were betrayed by my clothes and my accent. My only real friend was Ernest, a 'bad lot', an incorrigible dunce, but a poacher of genius. Ah, when it came to snaring rabbits, trapping blackbirds or catching trout from the river Ouche with his bare hands, Ernest had no equal! How many times, thanks to him, was I able to make a substantial improvement in the family meals! In exchange, my mother used to give him our old clothes and shoes. Everything fitted him superbly, and he wore our cast-offs indefinitely. Thanks to him, they seemed to become eternal.

Mushrooms were his speciality. He would have been able to find them under the schoolmaster's desk, and tasty ones, at that! He had no theoretical knowledge, but he had a sure and infallible instinct for telling the difference between the poisonous and the edible varieties. On one condition, though: if you wanted his advice, you mustn't show him your crop in a handkerchief or a basket. In such cases he would shake his head, refuse to pronounce, and admit his ignorance. Mushrooms were only recognizable on the ground where they grew, before anyone had touched them. Ernest was like that.

Fairy-ring champignons ... I remembered a field that sometimes became flooded, below the Fontaine Fermée – one of the two sources of the Ouche – which was called, I couldn't say why, Ganders Valley. I would have been willing to swear that at that very moment the mushrooms were forming their fairy rings in the thin grass covering that meagre soil.

I couldn't get to sleep, but fell into a sort of waking dream which took me back to those childhood years which after all are fairly short, although they constitute the basis of one's entire existence. Ganders Valley and its fairy-ring champignons, Ernest with his pockets full of lizards, insects, nests, eggs, knives, gadgets for catching fish or setting traps. It was thirty-five years since I had left all that behind me, yet it was so alive and so close. Wasn't there a lot of ingratitude in my having so totally neglected that village and those people who had surrounded and nourished my childhood during the dark years?

I got up. I was definitely not sleepy. I dressed, knowing in my heart of hearts, though not yet daring to formulate, the plan I was acting on. The Bentley was waiting in the underground garage, a sleepy, docile monster. It only had to be given the order and it would leap up out of its lair. I gave the order. The electronic gate slowly swung up. The engine hummed gently. The Avenue Foch was bathed in pallid light. I drove towards the ring road. It was half past two in the morning when I joined the Autoroute du Sud.

When I got to the Pouilly-en-Auxois exit, I hesitated. I had initially intended to press on to Beaune, then to head back to Montigny on the Route Nationale 470. But the names of the villages on the signs announcing the Pouilly exit sang so sweetly in my ear that I couldn't resist their appeal. Commarin, the village of the Burgundian writer-railwayman Henri Vincenot; Pont-de-Pany, where my maternal grandmother had lived as a child and where she was buried; Chazilly, where we went bathing, my brothers and I, in an artificial pond. So I left the autoroute, and at once more memories came jumping up into my face. There were even some that were second-hand, which concerned my parents or grandparents, I mean, and which I had heard evoked a hundred times in the family circle. Thus, as I started down the hill leading to Sainte-Sabine, I remembered the great massacre of geese my grandfather had perpetrated at the wheel of his Citroën B12 in 1926. When he stopped outside the chemist's in Bligny-sur-Ouche, my grandmother was amazed to see the car covered in white feathers. 'They'll be eating goose in Sainte-Sabine to-morrow,' said my grandfather with biblical simplicity. The dawn was whitening the eastern horizon as I slowly passed that same chemist's shop. What a lot of memories, what a lot of dead people!

It's two kilometres from Bligny to Montigny. Everything was still asleep when I entered the village. This was a relief to me. After an absence of so many years, I would have hated a triumphal entry at the wheel of my flashy car. The first thing I did was to go to Ganders Valley, by the Fontaine Fermée. I couldn't believe my eyes: a wood! Where before there had been undulating water meadows, there was now a little forest of regularly-planted alders. Actually, the idea of draining this swamp by planting it with trees was quite reasonable. But the presence, and above all the height, of these alders suddenly made me aware of the weight of the years. Well, yes, it takes less than thirty-five years to transform a plantation of saplings into a wood of fully-grown trees! I suddenly felt old, and already very far beyond 'the middle of the journey of our life' that Dante speaks of. And then I was disappointed. What about my fairy-ring champignons? Had I got up in the middle of the night and come all this way only to return empty-handed? Once more I searched my memories. At the top of La Balance, in the pastures of Bessey-en-Chaume, I remembered a little wood with an open space – open, yet sheltered by some overhanging larches. For the fairy ring champignon is so constituted that it needs air and light, but also the protection of a hedge, a wall, or a projecting corner of a wood.

So there I was, off again in my splendid automobile heading towards Beaune, up the hill called La Balance. After five kilometres you turn left into a little secondary road that leads to Crépey, and just before Bessey . . . Everything was there. When I got out of the car I rediscovered the slightly alpine atmosphere of those Burgundian heights (the Bessey-en-Chaume col is the highest point of the Autoroute du Sud), with its cylindrical grasses and its clumps of pines. My overhanging larches hadn't budged. And, true to expectation, the wrinkled mushrooms (*Marasmius oreades*), a whole colony of champignons, were there to greet me. I fetched the plastic bag I had thrown into the boot, and went to work as eagerly as if I were once more twelve years old. Was it because I had grown up? It seemed to me that the mushrooms I had picked in this very spot long ago were finer than those of today. Golden mists of the past, how you magnify the most insignificant things!

My full, heavy bag roused me from my dream. What was I going to do now? Drive away and go back to Paris? A joyless prospect. But then what? who? Ernest, of course! In all likelihood, my inspired poacher had no more stirred than the corner of the Bessey larch wood. It was six o'clock, and rosy-fingered dawn was rising behind the distant Crépey bell-tower. Just the right time to catch that man of the wild.

The Bentley purred like a fat cat as it rolled down La Balance.

When I reached the little inn that used to be kept by the Guérets, I turned left and crossed the bridge over the Ouche. Ernest's parents' house had certainly suffered some dilapidation, with its staircase all askew and its roof patched up like the seat of an old pair of pants, but it welcomed me as an old friend. I knocked at the door. A voice I immediately recognized asked: 'Who is it?' I gave my name. The door opened. 'So it's you, then?' Certainly he had changed a lot, and I am not sure whether, if I had passed this hirsute faun in the street, I should immediately have recognized my old pal. But on second thoughts, the metamorphosis of the lanky redhead with the razor-sharp gaze whom I had known into this moustachioed fox, his green eyes narrowed by irony – this metamorphosis seemed to follow the logic that requires the child to be father of the man. 'I came for some mushrooms,' I told him, holding out my bag, as if this explanation sufficed to justify my irruption after thirty-five years' silence. 'Mushrooms?' he said, casting a glance into my bag, 'ah, that's you all over!' And the whole of his sharpened face reflected intense amusement tempered by the indulgence called for by my case. 'Down, Briffaut!' A dog of some ill-defined breed, in which nevertheless the spaniel predominated, was passionately sniffing at my legs and my trouser-fly. 'Well, I was just going to have breakfast,' said Ernest. 'We'll add a mushroom omelette, if you like.' I did like, all the more so as I had had no dinner the previous day. He offered me a chair, sat down by a bucket and began to peel the mushrooms. I observed his room. It contained a whole collection of rustic and forest odds and ends: rabbit skins drying on frames, fishing-nets, cages, hampers, traps, scales for crayfish, an axe lying on a pile of logs, and I noted that the three guns in the wall-rack over the unmade bed were within reach of a man lying down. An ancestral custom, or inveterate suspicion?

'You live all alone?'

'Alone. My only master after God! You know I didn't get on so well with my father. I left. When he died, I came back to live with my mother. She died too, a few years ago, I don't remember how many. Didn't want to go to the hospice. Was quite right. Since then, no one. Alone with Briffaut. Isn't that right, Briffaut?'

The dog agreed with a wag of his tail.

'So just like that, you drove all night to come and pick some champignons?'

Strictly true, this absurdity called for another, which Ernest accepted without further objection:

'My wife is in Rio de Janeiro with my polo ponies. I was free.'

Free . . . True freedom – was it not here before my eyes? Hadn't my All Saints' Day champignons obliged me to discover it? Ernest had started out by my side on the bench of the primary school in this village. Then we were separated, and our divergent paths led me to a town house in the avenue Foch, and him to return to his point of departure, this tumbledown cottage where he was born, this house full of life and smells, here with his mongrel. I had fought hard to make my fortune, and I had succeeded. I had been through two divorces, and it was only our mutual interest in horses that still kept us together, my third wife and I. I had been round the world several times, from east to west and from west to east. What particularly impressed me was Ernest's total lack of curiosity about me. What I might have done with all that time quite simply didn't interest him. He hadn't budged a single metre. He was living today in the way he had lived as a child and adolescent. The monotony of his life, punctuated by the recurring seasons in which days were superimposed on days, and years on years, must have reduced to virtually nothing the thirty-five years – for me full to overflowing with adventures, both successful and unsuccessful – during which I had disappeared from his field of vision. And finally, it was I alone who had questions to ask him. The surprising thing was that he proved to be communicative, almost eloquent, this great loner, but I very soon noticed that although he seemed to be addressing his remarks to me, he was all the time exchanging glances with Briffaut, who was quite clearly his only real interlocutor. Robinson Crusoe on his desert island. He reminded me of him, with his sheepskin waistcoat and his reddish beard. And I? I was the captain of the first English ship in decades to reach the island, who was trying to enter into a dialogue with the goatherd. In actual fact I was trying to imagine what my life would have been like if, like him, I had stayed in these haunts of my childhood.

Faces came drifting through my memory. Annette Mazurier, for example. She was my puerile madonna. There was no better pupil in the village school, or even in the whole canton, so they said. At the age of twelve she was as serious-minded as a grown-up woman. Her little face, of angelic purity, might have seemed over-solemn had it not been for the fragility that was its saving grace. What had she become? A midwife? a magistrate? an abbess?

'Annette? Ah, la Mazurier? Ah, that poor girl, she has certainly had a rough time! True, she more or less asked for it. Can you imagine! She was seventeen, no more, when she got herself snared by a good-for-nothing who had just turned up from Dijon. A former parachutist who had distinguished himself in Indochina. At least that's what he said. He never stopped talking about his shady exploits. We all did our best to warn Annette off him. And anyway he made no bones about it: 'I'm a hoodlum.' It was what you might call written on his face. You only had to look at him. Annette was the only one who couldn't see it. She just wouldn't give an inch. Even when he admitted to her that he had a wife and kids in Dijon. Well, to cut a long story short, they got married. She had a first son, Pierrot they call him. She was expecting a second one when her handsome parachutist from Indochina disappeared. With the car, leaving her to pay the remaining instalments. A one-year-old child, another on the way, and debts. Not counting all those people who kept telling her spitefully: we told you so, you wouldn't listen, etc. She worked hard, did poor Annette. She had qualifications, so she became a schoolmistress. She even found another husband, a decent widower much older than her. She must have thought she'd seen the last of her hoodlum and that she wouldn't hear any more said about him. In one sense, yes. But there were her sons. The older one, he takes after his mother. No problem. But the other, he's the spitting image of his father. That Jeannot, he wasn't even eleven when he was brought home by a couple of gendarmes. Since then, he's been going more and more to the bad. Up till now his mother has been able to pay to get him out of his scrapes. But it won't last for ever . . .'

Annette, so sensible, so serious-minded that it began to look as if anyone who lived with her would find her a terrible bore, and that passion, that act of folly, physical no doubt, that threw her at the feet of the parachutist from Indochina. She must have known, intelligent as she was, that she was making a terrible mistake, but she had probably had enough of that reputation of hers, of being a model little girl, in which she was imprisoned. And the delayed-action revenge of the parachutist who disappeared but left in her womb the seed of another version of himself, which she wouldn't get rid of so quickly, seeing that he was her son. And with him, the first misfortune she had suffered was to be repeated.

The fire was roaring in the ancient kitchen range that was scored with numerous cracks. Would I still be able to obtain a blaze so quickly and without the slightest puff of smoke in the room? A whole art . . . Ernest threw what seemed to me an exorbitant quantity of mushrooms into a vast frying-pan. I also observed that he hadn't washed them, and I remembered an argument my mother had once had in this very place with a portly village woman who had come as an 'extra' to help with a big lunch party we were giving. She protested vigorously against the incomprehensible mania of townspeople for always wanting to drench everything in floods of water. She didn't give a fig for hygiene, and could see only one thing: when wet, all food, cooked or raw, is less tasty.

'And Edouard Lecoûtre? What became of Edouard?'

He was the mother's boy of the class. Timid, painstaking, always neat and tidy. A good pupil, too, because his mother made him do his homework every evening. His father had been killed in a road accident, and the widow Lecoûtre had taken strict control of their smallholding. About fifteen hectares, two horses, six cows, a hen-house, a rabbit-hutch, a handful of ducks dabbling in the pond – even so, this called for a farm hand and a maid. The widow had never been considered tenderhearted, but these two helpers very soon gave her a reputation for harshness and rapacity which nothing that happened later was to modify. They left, one after the other. She engaged some new ones. And each time it was the same old story: a money-grubbing virago of that sort belonged to another age, another civilization.

'And Edouard, in all that?'

This question provoked Ernest to hilarity.

'Ah, he certainly got the better of her, his bitch of a mother! Do you remember the Marélier girls, Ginette and Viviane?'

Did I remember them! Their parents were both total alcoholics. The children – I never knew exactly how many there were – used to put in episodic and picturesque appearances at school. More than once, one or the other bore the marks of such serious ill-treatment that the schoolmaster felt it his duty to inform the gendarmerie. Fierce discussions then ensued with the father, who turned up at the school, shouting and swearing that they weren't likely to see his children back there in a hurry.

'Well,' Ernest continued, 'what happens but Edouard gets besotted with Ginette Marélier! When he told his mother, she nearly killed him. Well, that's just a manner of speaking, because she'd always pampered her Edouard. But to go looking for a girl in that ghastly family! Never, never, never! Until the day when Ginette gets pregnant, and Edouard goes around everywhere bragging that he's responsible. Visit of old man Marélier to the widow Lecoûtre. I'd love to have seen that. All afternoon, it lasted. In the end they came to an agreement. Edouard would marry Ginette, but she'd never see her family again. Never. None of them. A complete and utter break. It was Viviane who told us all this. The Marélier family weren't even allowed to go to the wedding. And that's the truth. Afterwards, Viviane gave us regular news of her sister in the café in the square. At first, bread and water. Just occasionally coffee, milk. But above all, ah, above all, not a sou! The larder always double-locked. And the shopping – that, the women did together. But Ginette was only there to carry the parcels. She was like a stranger on the Lecoûtre farm. A servant who doesn't even get any wages! her sister used to shout out in the café.'

'But there was the child?'

'Oh yes, but the widow Lecoûtre had made up her mind: one child, no more. Strictly forbidden to have a second one! But that's where everything changed. A daughter, that's what Ginette had. They called her Alberte, what d'you think of that! And it didn't take Ginette any time at all to realize that this baby might possibly hold the key to her prison. Because right from the start, the terrible widow Lecoûtre melted like snow in the sun at the sight of her granddaughter. Absolutely gaga she was, over that baby! People who saw it couldn't believe their eyes. Nothing was too good for Alberte. Her grandmother's purse couldn't open wide enough in the toy shops or children's clothes shops in Beaune. At the same time she made her son and daughter-in-law work even harder, but Ginette was laughing up her sleeve and confidently awaiting the future.'

'The future?'

'Yes, because from the moment Alberte began to open her eyes she sized up the situation perfectly. She saw that her mother was a poor slave waiting to be freed. It didn't take long! At ten she had the best bicycle in the village, at fourteen her Vespa, at eighteen she had passed her driving test and was christening her Renault 4. While Edouard had never been allowed a car! At the same time the widow Lecoûtre was gradually losing control of the farm. Mother and daughter between them have seen to it that at this very moment she's in a cupboard waiting to be taken off to the old people's home in Bolleyne. That's love for you!'

We much enjoyed an enormous mushroom omelette washed down by a best-vintage Clos Vougeot. Decidedly, this Burgundy of my childhood is a province where people know how to live, even if here, as elsewhere, they are money-grubbers, and hard on drunkards and those weakened by a great love.

I went on automatically coming out with names as one by one they emerged from oblivion. The number of dead was frightening. Young Chambert, who never went anywhere without his tool-box and whose sole pleasure consisted in taking agricultural machines or moped engines to bits: blown sky-high by a German mine. He'd wanted to see what was inside it. The Mole, a tall, skinny girl with straight hair, so called because of her short-sightedness: cut down by an attack of peritonitis, which antibiotics would have cured two years later. As for the Guérets, the couple who for fifty years had run the tiny inn located like a boundary stone at the head of the bridge, their respective ages at the time I left quite clearly ruled out the possibility of their still being there. Ernest told me that they died within forty-eight hours of each other, she first, then the old boy, no doubt appalled by the two days he lived without his wife. And there were those who, like me, had left the village and never been heard of since, but on the other hand there were a few new arrivals.

Of the latter, I knew one, Vladimir, known as Vava, who was an accordionist in a Dijon brasserie at the time. He was the brother of a farmer's wife from these parts, Honorine Certain, a capable woman, as generous as nature and surrounded by a teeming brood of children. Old Certain looked like the warrior on the Celtique cigarette-packet, a giant with long blond moustaches. A superb family who inspired respect and friendship. Vava used to appear for brief visits, always with his instrument, with its beautiful ivory keys, and his air of the town-dweller out of his element among these clodhoppers. I had detested him from the very first, this dapper little fellow in his bum-freezer with his chest thrown out, his flashy ties and pointed, two-tone, high-heeled shoes. He played at being the young aristocratic fop, bewildered by the smells and sounds of a rustic household, and all those good people laughed with genuine amusement at his commercial-traveller's jokes and puns.

Then misfortune had struck. There had been an exchange of fire on the road, between a German column and a group of maquisards. The next day at dawn a Ukrainian Wehrmacht regiment laid siege to the village and ransacked the houses. The men were shut up in the church. The Certain family bore the brunt of that accursed day. The father, the farm hand and the two oldest daughters were first isolated, and then taken out into the forest. Everyone thought they were going to be shot there. But it was only to make them bury nine maquisards who had been killed during the mopping-up operation that had taken place earlier. But they didn't come back, because they were first put in prison in Dijon, and then deported to Buchenwald.

A few days later, as if life was in duty bound to counter the assaults of death with an act of defiance, Honorine Certain brought twins into the world. This was beautiful, it was sublime, but it made the situation at the farm even more dramatic. At this point Vava turned up, more frizzed and brilliantined than ever, his accordion, with its beautiful ivory keys, slung over his shoulder. And Vava had ditched his bum-freezer, he had dumped his pointed shoes, his flashy tie and even his beautiful instrument. He had rolled up his sleeves to reveal his puny, townee's biceps, and begun to cope with all the work that had to be done in spring on the farm threatened with ruin by the loss of the *patron*, the farm hand and the two oldest daughters.

'And now?'

'Now? He's still there, is Vava. You can go and see him. A year after the Liberation, old Certain and his two daughters came back. As for the farm hand, we never heard of him again. But Certain was mortally affected. A wreck. He took to drink. Almost every day Vava had to go and fetch him from the café and put him to bed. He died in the fifties. Vava never left. He's become a real old-time farm labourer with his sister. His nephews and nieces respect him as their father. He even grew a moustache, to imitate his brother-in-law. Sometimes, of a Sunday, everyone insists on him bringing out his accordion. He has a go. But he says he can't play properly any more, with his big peasant fingers. That's life for you!'

It only remained for me to enquire after my childhood home, the presbytery that had been a refuge in my war years.

'The presbytery? Ah, that's a sorry business! You know that, like the church, it belongs to the commune. When your family left after the war it was let to some local people. They never wanted to do any repairs to it. Of course not: it didn't belong to them. The local council got obstinate, too. Simply said that the rent was too low to justify their spending any money. So one fine day part of the roof fell in. And the tenants had to leave. They even got compensation from the commune. Since then, nobody, nothing. It's falling into ruin.'

The ruin of that pious and reassuring big house because nobody loved it . . . Once again a kind of remorse gripped me. Isn't it a sin to forget one's most cherished past to such a degree?

'Why don't we go and have a look?'

'If you really want to!'

The dog had immediately understood that we were going out, and was already running up and down in front of the door. Ernest took his cap and a springy hazel branch that was lying about. The hat and stick without which gentlemen of old never left the house, I thought fleetingly. All he needs are the gloves. He'd certainly have had them if it had been cold!

We were greeted by a beautiful autumn morning. A warm, moist, westerly breeze was caressing the russet manes of the trees. A flock of geese went by, jabbering noisily. The last swallows spaced themselves out on the electric cables like notes on a music stave. Briffaut went off half-heartedly in pursuit of a cat, which disappeared into a basement window. How calm and set in its rightful place everything here seemed! Could passions and intrigues be lurking, as they do everywhere, beneath the old moss-covered tiles of these roofs?

We were already walking along the dry-stone wall of the presbytery garden and we could count the gaps that allowed free access to it. A pathetic garden overgrown with brambles, nettles and sorrel, no longer what they call a curé's garden but just a bit of waste ground. When we went in, we put a couple of dormice to flight.

'They'll soon be hibernating,' Ernest observed.

I noticed the disappearance of the two immense fir trees in which I used to spend the warm summer hours, cradled by the soughing of the wind in their tiered branches. I would have thought that they too were eternal, indestructible. Destroyed by time, killed by men – my beautiful giants . . .

The presbytery was open to all the winds that blew. From the staircase, you could see the sky through a gaping crack in the roof. The rotted floors gave beneath our feet. The windows were hanging out of their frames. Only the main structure was still sound. But only just! I remembered then that we used to have to get our water from a pump in the courtyard, and the lavatory consisted of a shed built over a pit in the garden.

And yet my imagination was at work. I was making plans. Here a bathroom, as big as a living room, with a large bay window looking out on to the mountain. There a monumental fireplace where we would burn the 'estovers' – the allocation of communal wood to which every inhabitant is entitled. I rapturously remembered some Burgundian winters that were so cold and so dry that in order to explain them the meteorologists talked of a corridor that must bring the polar winds directly down into the region. But the thing that excited me most was the potential of the outbuildings. I chose the site of the garage for the cars, of a stable for my horses, and a kennel for the hounds. I would also have a kitchen garden, a rabbit-hutch, a pigeon-loft and an enclosure for the pheasants. As the two sources of the Ouche meet in the garden, it would be easy to have a tank dug for trout of irreproachable freshness. Every morning I would go to market without leaving my own grounds: lettuces, eggs, chicken, rabbit, fish . . . I made a mental calculation of what it would cost to make this beautiful dream come true. The money would be the least of my problems. Wasn't it

La Fontaine who wrote that? It's true that he also wrote *The Milk-maid and Milk-pail.*

'Do you think the commune would sell it to me?'

'The presbytery? I'd be surprised. There's no one more pig-headed than the mayor.'

'Who is he?'

'Amaury, his name is. Hector Amaury. He used to be a builder. Lives on nothing. Can't stand change. But we can always go and see him.'

We went. I immediately realized that the couple we formed was not calculated to reassure the old curmudgeon: Ernest's reputation must have left something to be desired, and as for me, the news of my irruption in that too-beautiful, Paris-registered car had clearly already gone the rounds of the village. However hard I tried to present myself as a child of the region and recall my years in the village school, Amaury stood squarely in his doorway and gave no sign of inviting us in.

'It's about renting the presbytery,' Ernest finally ventured.

'It's not for rent,' Amaury said curtly.

'In actual fact,' I said timidly, 'with all the work it needs, I would really prefer to buy it. Because you see . . .'

'It's not for sale,' Amaury interrupted me. 'And anyway, that house isn't habitable in the state it's in.'

'That's just it, I've had a quick look at it. I'm prepared to be responsible for all the necessary work . . .'

This clearly shook the former builder. He stepped back a fraction, as if he was going to ask us in. Unfortunately, though, I added:

'To restore it properly, which I would like to do, would take between two and three million . . .'

Amaury jumped when he heard these figures.

'Two or three million? You think you can get away with that? But just the work on the roof would need at least three times as much as that!'

He laughed scornfully at the penury he thought he had uncovered. These Parisians, they give themselves airs with their solid-gold cars, and then they haven't got a sou to spend on their houses! Once again he stood squarely in his doorway. No question now of asking me in. There was an obvious misunderstanding. I ruined my chances for good by clearing it up:

'Monsieur le maire, when I say two to three million I'm not talking in centimes. I'm talking in francs. In new francs!'

'Two to three hundred million?'

His mouth fell open in stupefaction. His eyes widened in horror.

'Well yes, what do you expect? To make that ruin comfortable, to build a garage, stables, a house for the caretakers, and all the rest of it . . .'

Amaury was still staring at me, appalled.

'Two to three hundred million? You must be mad! You want to revolutionize the village? You want to . . . you want to . . .'

He was speechless. Finally he hammered out:

'The presbytery, as I've already told you, is neither for rent nor for sale!'

He turned his back on us and went into his house. I looked at Ernest, who was chuckling into his moustache. We headed back to his house and to the Bentley, quietly waiting at the foot of the steps.

'You went about it too quickly,' he said. 'You ought to have come and settled here. Made yourself known, beaten about the bush, advanced your pawns patiently.'

Patience! There's a virtue that is not my strong point. It seems to me on the contrary that all my successes have been due to my impatience, to the rapidity of my calculations and of the actions that have followed them. Being quick. In business as in love. But isn't that also the cause of all my failures?

*   *   *

Three days later I went back to Roissy to meet my wife and see my ponies through customs.

As we were putting her suitcases into the boot of the Bentley, she came upon a plastic bag in which a handful of mushrooms were in the last stages of putrefaction.

47

'What's that?' she asked.

I threw the whole thing into one of the car-park bins.

'It's nothing. Fairy-ring champignons from Montigny. You wouldn't understand.'

She didn't insist. She has always respected the mystery of the years of origin, those fabulous times when not only did we not know each other but she wasn't even born.

Théobald or
The Perfect Crime

A fifteen-year gap – is that enough to put you out of the picture? I was desperately trying to persuade myself that it was, but I wasn't having much success in fending off my feeling of guilt when I read in my paper the circumstances of the death of Professor Théobald Bertet. Everything seemed to prove that he had been murdered, and that the two guilty parties were his wife, Thérèse, and her lover, a certain Harry Pink. The thing is that for me, the name Thérèse Bertet takes me back to an adventure that was both bitter and passionate, the memory of which is exquisite, for it is part and parcel of my youth.

I was studying for an arts degree, and to make ends meet I had assumed the modest functions of a supervisor in the municipal college in Alençon. Théobald Bertet was in charge of the two first forms, and he should have looked down on me from the heights of his success in the highest competitive examination for teachers, the *agrégation*. But he didn't, for actually no one was less disdainful than he. It's hard to imagine a more colourless individual, a more bowed figure, a more miserable, lacklustre wretch. Luckily for him, the children who fell to his lot were very young and his classes were traditionally among the easiest, for adolescents of the 'awkward age' would have made short work of him. Perhaps he had had this painful experience at the outset of his career? I remember his hesitations one day when we were talking shop, and discussing the various relationships that can be established between master and pupils. No doubt my remarks – which I have forgotten – were optimistic? I don't know. But I can still see him shaking his head with a wounded air and repeating: 'Oh no, children aren't good, you know, they're savages. They only have to feel they're stronger than you.' And yet, while Bertet inspired me with pity mingled with repugnance (at my age I still felt close to those 'savage' children), it was impossible for me to despise him, because you only had to encourage him to emerge from his silence and he displayed an astonishing and very subtle erudition, having his Latin and Greek classics at his fingertips, talking knowledgeably of Romanesque architecture and Baroque painting, atonal music and the *Nouveau Roman*. At such times he gave you the painful impression that you and your like, the course of events and the reign of money and force, belonged to a vulgar, ignoble domain whereas he walked alone and entranced in a secret garden where everything is refinement and transparence.

Now, by an incredible paradox, this shadow of a man had a wife of radiant beauty, health, and appetite for living and loving. There was a striking contrast between this young Walkyrie with a chest like the prow of a ship and the grey, drab half-portion she trailed behind her. Such cases are more frequent than people realize. Some women's will to power is only satisfied by a feeble husband, as pliable as an empty glove.

I was young, naïve, and enterprising. On Sunday mornings I could be seen training on the school sports ground. I made up for the humiliating image of the lowly supervisor I gave the pupils by outclassing the oldest ones at the hundred metres or the high jump. As they all dreamed of the beautiful Thérèse Bertet, I decided, as much from real desire as from conceit, to make her my mistress. My enterprise succeeded with ease, but my vanity was such that this didn't even surprise me. What did surprise me, on the other hand, was Thérèse's habit of including her husband in all our tête-à-têtes. 'Like that,' she reasoned, 'no one will be able to say anything.' No doubt. Being a slave to stereotypes, though, as young men often are, it pained me to recognize myself as one of the classic boulevard-comedy trio: the woman, the lover and the complacent husband. Yet it should have been easy for me to detect in our relationship some curious, profoundly worrying features which conferred an incomparable originality on it. But I was blind to the nature of our affair. It was only with hindsight and after reflection that I realized its complexity.

Intellectually, then, it wasn't ideal. Physically, we produced sparks. This could have made up for the rest if a third factor hadn't arisen to complicate the whole issue. My new friends cost me dear, very dear, considering how little I earned as a humble supervisor. It seemed to go without saying that whenever we went out together, I paid. Thérèse very soon swept aside the timid show Bertet put up when the bill arrived. What was more, she had borrowed from me the money she needed to buy a car, on the pretext that the instalments on hire-purchase were daylight robbery. I had had to liquidate my savings-account book, having decided that since I was, as they say, on a winning streak, I might as well throw my bonnet over the windmill. What remained of my savings would pay for the journey to Greece I was planning for the holidays.

Our passionate love affair lasted for a term, a unit of time dear to teachers' hearts. Thérèse and I cultivated the adulterous hours between five and seven in my little student's room. Until the day when the inexplicable happened.

Between five and seven, in fact, while I was gloriously straddling my Walkyrie, the door opened. How the devil could I have forgotten to lock it? But had I actually forgotten? Hadn't another hand unlocked it? Théobald's silhouette was outlined in the doorway. As we were in semi-darkness, we could only see him against the light. Nothing more wretchedly caricatural than that body which always seemed to be in profile even when you were facing it – with its dangling arms, its right shoulder higher than the other, its oversized head leaning leftwards, as if dragged down by its own weight.

He stood there for quite a while, as if in a daze, an interminable length of time during which Thérèse's powerful thighs imprisoned me in a grip that prevented me from moving. Then he slowly shut the door again, and we heard his shuffling steps retreating.

Thérèse made a dash for her clothes. In two minutes she was dressed and ready to leave. 'He's suicidal,' she stammered. 'He'd be quite capable of committing suicide.' She rushed out.

The next morning the headmaster, Monsieur Julienne, summoned me to his study. He was a shrewd, well-groomed man who affected a free-and-easy manner. He treated me with amused nonchalance, and alluded to the spring, my youth, and my success with the ladies.

'Only you see,' he added, 'you went a little too far. One of your colleagues has complained of your behaviour towards his wife, who has confirmed her husband's allegations. They produced other evidence. Now an educational establishment must protect itself against this kind of scandal. What an example for the children! In a town like Alençon . . . the teachers' council . . . the parents' association . . .'

In short, he felt obliged to ask me to go and exercise my talents as a supervisor-seducer in another establishment.

So I would have got off with no more than a move if it hadn't been for the money I had lent them for the car. I could only claim it back from Bertet, whom I had so sorely wronged, in courteous and moderate terms. This was the object of a meticulously polite letter I sent him. And as troubles never arrive singly, I must – once again! – have left the door to my little room open, because when I was collecting up my clobber before leaving, I could find no trace of the roll of banknotes I had hidden in my underclothes, and which was intended for my holiday in Greece.

I was young, the adventure had left me with some grandiose memories and, my goodness, there's a price to be paid for everything. Nevertheless, I harboured a considerable grudge against the Bertet couple.

Théobald answered my letter. His consisted of more sheets of paper covered in illegible handwriting than my patience could bear. The only thing that mattered to me was that it did not contain an accompanying cheque. I glanced through it with a wrathful eye, then tossed it with other papers into the bottom of a drawer.

A few months later I met a former colleague from the Alençon school.

'The Bertets?' he said. 'Haven't you heard? You remember our elegant headmaster, Monsieur Julienne? Well, at the end of the third term – that unit of time dear to teachers' hearts – Monsieur Bertet caught his wife in the man's arms. Unfortunately he had the deputy headmaster with him. The affair caused quite a stir. Bertet complained to the regional authorities. What made everything worse was that the scandal had taken place on the school premises. You can imagine a thing like that in a town . . .'

'Like Alençon,' – I took the words out of his mouth – 'with the teachers' council and the parents' association, etc. Yes, I know all that.'

'In short, the wretched Bertet was transferred with great ceremony to a lycée in the Paris suburbs. And you want me to tell you what I think?'

'I'll tell you what *I* think – I should be surprised if it wasn't the same. That Thérèse is a hell of a race-course filly, and at the rate she's going, running her love affairs in tandem with her husband's career, I can see him before very long as a professor at the Sorbonne or the Collège de France. Not to speak of the fortune she will have gleaned along the way, because, unlike a stone, a rolling woman does gather moss . . .'

* * *

Well, that was fifteen years ago. I had heard no more of the Bertets until I came across a sensational report in my newspaper. Apparently, Bertet had not had the brilliant career for which Thérèse's performances had destined him. Death had caught up with him on the eve of his retirement from the post of headmaster of a Paris lycée. As for the accomplice, a certain Harry Pink, he was a young English student-teacher who had had a temporary job in the same lycée. All this had a tremendous air of *déja-vu* for me, apart from the fact that a man was dead and there were two accused behind bars. I also noticed another difference. The paper had printed photographs of the three protagonists. Bertet had hardly changed since our last interview. It's true that he had probably never looked young. He was one of those men who from year to year become the old man they have fundamentally always been since the age of twenty. I liked the look of the young Englishman, because I inevitably identified him with the naïve young man I had been when I'd had dealings with that odd couple. But he hadn't been so lucky as I. What a frightful predicament his amours with Thérèse had got him into! As for her, her picture shattered me. The muscular Walkyrie I had known had turned into a powerful, ample lioness. Majestic, calm, and sure of herself, oh yes, but her cheeks and neck, and also a shadow under her chin, showed that she was no longer in full bloom, but already on the way to becoming overblown. And it was above all her gaze that had changed. It had lost that fiery defiance and appetite for living that had been its charm. What could be read in it was at best anxious anticipation, at worst resigned fatigue. And yet my Walkyrie was still quite something, and it was easy to understand how a very young man had allowed himself to be embraced by those fleshy arms and those massive thighs.

The circumstances of Bertet's death, which at first had seemed to suggest an accident – as Thérèse maintained – on examination led to her being implicated and charged with murder. Bertet had in fact died in his bath, electrocuted by his electric razor. But the inquest revealed that he only ever shaved with a safety razor – which was found – and the appliance that had caused his death was of the type 'for ladies', and belonged to Thérèse. But the most serious evidence against Thérèse and her lover was a letter that Bertet had written to his sister a few days before his death, and which she lost no time in producing. In this letter, Bertet accused his wife and her young Englishman of trying to do away with him. Thérèse had made him take out an insurance policy which would make his widow a millionairess if he were to die. He claimed he had already twice by chance escaped accidents they had organized, which should have been mortal. In short, he warned his sister that if he were to die accidentally, it would in fact be murder committed by Thérèse and her lover.

Once again, I could only consider the whole affair in the light of my memories, and by identifying myself with Thérèse's young lover. Could such a misfortune have happened to me fifteen years ago? Without the slightest doubt. On the other hand, I was unable to recognize the Thérèse I had known in the murderess the entire press described with such grim complacency. Passionately sensual, yes, furiously self-interested, certainly, but totally amoral – that was less sure. Because as I see it, love of life doesn't exist without an instinctive rejection of certain actions, in particular actions leading to death. Thérèse was a greedy woman, her avidity was not burdened with the slightest scruple, but illness and blood made her jib like a horse that catches the smell of the slaughterhouse. I remembered now her revulsion when I once mentioned the case of a colleague who discovered she was pregnant and had an abortion. 'Not me – never!' she had muttered, flattening her two hands on her stomach, as though to protect it from murderers in white coats. And something else she had said came back to me now. It was the day when her husband had caught us together and then fled, leaving us entangled with each other. 'He's suicidal,' she had said, as she gathered up her clothes. Was it suicide? But in a case of violent death, surely, after accident and murder, suicide is the third possibility to be considered?

Day after day, with the press raking over every aspect of the Bertet affair and vying with each other to blacken Thérèse's character, I could see it gradually moving towards a major conviction. Yet a memory was stirring in me and trying, so it seemed, to emerge from the oblivion in which it was buried. A letter. The letter Bertet had written me shortly after I had left Alençon. Exasperated at finding it didn't contain the cheque I had been expecting in repayment of the money I had lent the couple, I had glanced rapidly through all those pages scrawled over in barely legible handwriting. To hell with the garrulous crook! It wasn't a dissertation I wanted! Asking myself now what the letter had contained, just two words floated up to the surface of my memory: suicide and revenge. Yes, it was a question of nothing but that in those pages. As for the rest ... it was shrouded in darkness. But suicide and revenge – that seemed likely to throw a strange light on Bertet's death.

What had I done with the letter? This wasn't a totally nonsensical question, for I have a mania for keeping everything, especially letters, even the most unimportant ones. Unfortunately, though, my penchant for keeping everything doesn't go hand in hand with a sense of order, and my papers accumulate in shapeless bundles which I lose in the course of my frequent moves.

I started to search. The more time went by, the more my chances of finding the letter diminished, and the more I convinced myself that it constituted a piece of vital evidence in the case. I spent whole days of feverish activity, anguish, and fury with myself. Incidentally, there is nothing more depressing than immersing yourself in old papers, old letters, messages so out-of-date that they have become incomprehensible. What ashes, what lapses of memory, what vain projects, what dead love affairs! It was as if I were exhuming and searching the corpse of the young man I had been, and while he was sometimes touching in his naïveté, I have to admit that he didn't always smell good. Finally, with a roar of triumph, I found Bertet's letter in the manuscript of a novel I had begun, abandoned, gone back to, and then definitively forgotten. As I read those pages covered in Bertet's microscopic handwriting, I told myself that this authentic document in itself constituted a novel a thousand times more moving and profound than anything I might have invented, and that, no doubt, is the typical thought of the non-novelist. But what does it matter today?

My dear young colleague,
The difference in age between us is the only excuse for this letter. I wouldn't know how to write to a man of my own age who was Thérèse's lover. You, at least, could be my son, if

not Thérèse's. This circumstance disarms my grievances, at least those I have against you, for so far as Thérèse, my mother, my father, life in general, etc., are concerned, the charges I could bring against them are no doubt inexhaustible.

I am a weak, unlucky man, as you will easily have noticed. I must have been born feet first, protesting and struggling against the violence they were doing me in bringing me into the world. I have never reconciled myself to existing, and I long to return to the nothingness I should never have left. 'O Lord, I was infinitely tranquil and non-existent in nothingness. I was wrenched out of that state and hurled into a strange carnival.' Monsieur Teste was speaking with the amused detachment of the great aesthete. Personally, I have never considered it a strange carnival, but something far more like sinister buffoonery. I won't tell you about my sickly and humiliated childhood. From the time I was in the kindergarten, playgrounds were places of torment for me. The grotesque thing is that I have never been able to escape them, as I became a teacher. Certainly not by vocation, good God no! By anti-vocation, rather! I mean, through my inability to do anything else, to risk venturing into any other domain than the scholastic. I failed the agrégation exam several times, but finally passed – through seniority, as it were – the poor man's agrégation, the agrégation de grammaire. By restricting me to the youngest classes, this at least protected me from the adolescents whose diabolical aggressiveness I only once had to suffer, when replacing a colleague. I still remember with horror that teenage class which I only had for one term, but whose barracking left me every evening exhausted, distraught, drunk with disgust at the idea of having to re-immerse myself in that cloaca the next day. I write this for your guidance, in case you have to continue in this career. I believe that a master has only one chance of getting himself accepted and of standing up to twenty or thirty boys and girls of between fourteen and seventeen, and that is by participating in some way in the kind of erotic intoxication characteristic of that age. It is probably possible to achieve this through demagogic connivance. But in this very peculiar domain there are some more spicy successes which imply playing a provocative game with the girls and indulging in a considerable dose of homosexuality with the boys. The most important thing, though, is to become a kind of adult sexual interlocutor for them, someone irreplaceable, for they will not find the equivalent anywhere, and certainly not in their parents. Of this, I am totally incapable. Between me and my teenage class there was nothing but reciprocal and unequivocal rejection. The next term, luckily, I was back with my first forms and their innocence.

My relations with Thérèse were what they were bound to be. She had married an instrument. She used it to make herself a place in the sun. Her parents were dazzled when she became the wife of a civil servant-cum-scholar. She shared their naïve admiration for one of the representatives of a social class she considered superior. This explains a bizarre habit which has always embarrassed me, but which I have never managed to change. As you will have observed, I quite naturally addressed her as tu. But in spite of all my pleading, she has never stopped calling me vous. In so doing, she was stressing – whether intentionally or not – both this social distance and the difference in our ages. Eleven years isn't so very much. But I have never been really young, and as for her – youth radiates from her whole body, from her every movement, from her mouth, and above all from her eyes. Thérèse! How I loved her! Passionately, painfully. And how gauche, ludicrous and vulnerable I have been in the face of her terrible assurance with other people! Without meaning to, by a word, by a gesture that came naturally to her, she would ruffle me, bruise me, make me bleed. One day she mortally wounded me, yes, even though it is a deferred death whose date I cannot foresee. We were newly-weds, 'a young couple' – if this expression can be applied to such a strange pair. I don't remember in what context, but I began to speak of the child we might have. She suddenly froze, and gazed at me as if she were seeing me for the first time. 'A child? With you?' She was assessing me, weighing me up, and there was such scorn in her look that I stood up and fled, unable to bear any more.

A child and life, the pursuit of life, survival itself – these are closely related ideas. To my mind, the arrival of a child – like my love for Thérèse – was an anchor that would save me from my old obsession with suicide. This door to salvation had just been brutally slammed. Thérèse's first 'affair' plunged me a little further into my dark night. I should probably have foundered, had I not suddenly felt a strange, macabre energy filling me and giving my life a new flavour. Oh, a bitter, acrid flavour, but a strong one, and of a nature to make me look to the future: I had just discovered jealousy and the thirst for revenge, which are inseparable, being the action and the passion of the same heart. Yes, I was deceived, rejected, wounded, but I would have my revenge, and for that I had to live.

But revenge myself for what, and on whom? My incurable wound was caused by Thérèse's refusal to have a child by me. My vindictive passion is centred on this idea of a child. It is not very original, I agree. If traditional societies punish female adultery so ferociously, it is because of the child whose identity it compromises. No doubt I must have a tradition-alist sensitivity. I shall never accept it, never, do you understand me, if Thérèse has a child by anyone but me. I have forgiven you, because your temporary liaison will leave no trace. But you know, if it had been otherwise, you would have had everything to fear – and Thérèse with you – from my despair. She knows this. She takes all the necessary precautions. But even more than the average woman, she has an irrepressible maternal vocation. The day she obeys this call, I shall kill myself. But believe me, I shall not go *under alone. My corpse, like a stone tied to their necks, will drag down Thérèse, her lover, and the detestable fruit of their fornication.*

Were these lines clear enough? Were they sufficient proof that Bertet had committed suicide and done everything possible to make his death look like murder? To be convinced of this, one last piece of evidence was needed.

I got in touch with the lawyer acting for the couple whom the press called 'the diabolical lovers'. I sent him Bertet's letter. He immediately had Thérèse examined, and it was found that she was indeed pregnant. She had confessed her condition to Bertet, without suspecting that she was pressing the red button that would trigger off a series of catastrophes. Bertet had at the same time killed himself and revenged himself. He thought he was killing four birds with one stone. Only he had forgotten the over-explicit letter written to a young colleague fifteen years previously. Intellectuals are like that. Their inordinate proclivity for words and writing often compromises their best-laid plans.

Thérèse's case was dismissed for lack of evidence. After she was released with Harry Pink, the first thing she did was phone to thank me. True, I had saved their bacon! Nevertheless, when with her characteristic insouciance she invited me to come and have a glass of champagne to celebrate this happy outcome, I refused. Perhaps, if she still remembered me in a year's time, I might become the child's godfather? I made this dilatory suggestion, and it was enthusiastically accepted. And that was the last I heard of the matter.

Pyrotechnics or
The Commemoration

My publisher had told me: 'You must get out of Paris, or you'll never finish your manuscript. I have a little dream house in Monteux, near Carpentras, with a swimming pool and a patio. You don't know anyone there. You'll have perfect peace. A de luxe monk, if you see what I mean. And don't come back until you have *It should be eaten cold* ready for the printer.' Because I had already told him the subject of my next thriller, a sinister tale of vengeance protracted throughout a whole lifetime, linking two people, both prisoners of the same initial act, the one impelled by the imperious duty to take his revenge, the other resigned, knowing he will not escape it, awaiting the retributory blow, as everyone awaits death, but simply knowing from whom it will come, and why. It seemed to me that the action should take place in the provinces, indeed in a rural setting, among people who have lived there all their lives and have always known one another; and that the initial act and the necessity for revenge it had engendered should be common knowledge. Everyone knew. Everyone was waiting. And this common knowledge made the revenge all the more necessary, all the more fatal.

Such was the skeleton plot – just how skeletal I had, as far as possible, concealed from my publisher so as not to drive Saint-Germain-des-Prés to despair and compromise the advance he had allowed me to hope for – with which one fine July morning I took the train for Avignon. From there, a bus was to take me in less than an hour to Monteux, not far from Carpentras.

The house lived up to all expectations. Like many old

Provençal dwellings, it had very few openings on to the exterior, as the natives traditionally consider the sun and the wind to be deadly scourges. On the other hand, an interior courtyard with a single jasmine plant – the famous patio – looked like a miniature cloister and invited one to solitary, meditative strolls. Twice a day Sidonie, a buxom local woman, turned up and saw to the house and to my meals, but above all she constituted the indispensable 'medium' between this unknown community and myself, for from the very first evening it became abundantly clear that the splendid isolation my publisher had promised me was totally illusory.

I was tired after the journey, and I intended to go to bed early. However, no sooner had I got between the sheets, of the kind most conducive to sleep, than a tremendous series of explosions shook the house and a light as bright as day filled the windows. Naturally, I immediately darted out on to the terrace. And there I watched the most beautiful firework display I had ever seen. Sky rockets and Bengal lights, fountains of flame and girandoles set the night ablaze for a good quarter of an hour. Back in my room I vainly searched my diary to find out what on earth this riot could be celebrating. It was 25 July – the feast-day of Saint Anne. But what interest did she hold for the inhabitants of Monteux, to the extent of attracting such brilliant homage?

Sidonie explained the mystery the next morning. She began by disconcerting me, though, as she seemed to be unaware of the fireworks that had so intrigued me. Even though she lived nearby, she had apparently not noticed anything. I was staggered. But I finally understood that these conflagrations were such a common occurrence in Monteux that its inhabitants no longer took any notice of them. For the town's main industry is the Ruggieri pyrotechnics factory, which owns an open space two hundred metres from the house, where it demonstrates its wares on request to any customers who happen to be passing through. So these displays only concern strangers. No Monteulais would stoop to paying the slightest attention to them.

No Monteulais, perhaps, but as a Parisian and a novelist, I

found this factory extremely interesting and most picturesque, and I spared no effort to obtain an interview with its managing director. I introduced myself, then, as a writer from Paris desirous of gathering material on pyrotechnics in general, and the Ruggieri works in particular, for a forthcoming book I was working on. True, nothing had been further from my thoughts on my arrival in the locality than fireworks, but a manuscript is like a plant growing deep down in the ground, whose roots nourish it on everything the soil has to offer. I had a vague feeling that pyrotechnics was beginning to haunt my future thriller.

Monsieur Capolini welcomed me with the assiduities of the professional who is flattered that a distinguished ignoramus should come from Paris to learn at his feet. Nevertheless, he talked so well and so brilliantly about fireworks that at times he seemed to become a firework himself. I have more than once come across this sort of total contamination of a man by his profession – a woman pork-butcher sculpted out of lard, a peasant kneaded out of earth and manure, a banker who resembles a safe, an equestrian with a neighing laugh. Capolini's hands were all the time turning into rockets, star-bursts, jets of fire or whirling Catherine wheels. His eyes seemed perpetually dazzled by some enchanting display.

'Strange and admirable craft!' he exclaimed, 'whose raw material is the explosion. Yes, Monsieur, we make concoctions here that all detonate. I have always adored the word detonate. It contains '*tonnerre*' – thunder – and astonishment. And we make ourselves masters of this detonation in order to displace it in space and delay it in time. We compose a detonating mixture which, instead of exploding here and now, will explode elsewhere and later. For example, in Paris, on the eve of the Fourteenth of July. But that's not all. This external displacement in time and space must also contain an internal dimension: the rocket has to inscribe its trajectory in the sky, and for that to happen the explosion must extend over a period of several seconds. You see, Monsieur, the whole of pyrotechnics comes down to a fight against the *hic et nunc*. Delay and display – these are the two imperatives of the pyrotechnic art.'

He led me out of his office and took me over to a curious village of little houses made of lightweight materials.

'An explosion *hic et nunc*, here and now,' he went on, 'would simply be an accident, a catastrophe. And if by some misfortune an explosion actually took place, everything has been done to limit its effects so far as is humanly possible. Look at these workshops. The slightest combustion would blow them to smithereens. And as you can see, the working teams have been reduced to the absolute minimum: two men, never more. You haven't any matches or a lighter on you?'

'No, I don't smoke.'

'Forgive me – it's our golden rule. Much like the rule of silence in a Trappist monastery.'

He pushed a door open and we entered one of the workshops. There were big metal containers full of different kinds of powder, bundles of cardboard tubes, pots of glue, rolls of paper. And two men in grey overalls sitting on opposite sides of a table, engaged in the least serious-minded work in the world: with scoops rather like teaspoons, and in an obviously predetermined order, they were pouring small quantities of powders into tubes which were constricted at the bottom by a clay choke. A scoopful of grey powder, a cardboard disc, a scoopful of green powder, a cardboard disc, a scoopful of black powder, etc.

Capolini walked around the room with the elegant nonchalance of a lion-tamer among his beasts. He took the stopper off a cylindrical container, ran a white powder through his fingers and announced: 'Sulphate of strontium: purple flame.' Then he went on to another receptacle: 'Iron filings: incandescent flowers.' Then, touching some sealed drums with his finger, he said: 'Zinc: blue flame. Saltpetre: golden droplets. Mica flake: golden rain. Barium salts: brilliant green. Copper carbonate: blue-green flame. Colophony: orange-coloured flame. Arsenic sulphide: brilliant white.' Then he came and sat down beside me, playing with an empty rocket.

'As you see, it has a choked orifice at its base. At that lower level, the powder is a fuse composition which forces gases through the hole under pressure, creating the upward thrust of the rocket. The cap is placed on top of the fuse composition. This is a charge of fine powder designed to expel the garniture from the cone of the rocket chamber at the moment when it reaches the zenith of its trajectory. This garniture is the rocket's *raison d'être*. Inside it are stars and droplets of light, flowers and cascades of fire. But I must tell you yet another secret. If the rocket were to be exactly as I have just described it, it would not blossom forth, it would not rise up into the sky, it wouldn't even leave the ground. Yes, Monsieur, such is the marvellous mystery of this object. Let me tell you: like women, like violins, a rocket has a soul. A soul without which it would remain extinct and earthbound. What is the soul of the rocket? I couldn't show it to you. A soul cannot be shown. The soul of the rocket is quite simply a cavity – the 'gallery' – made in its centre in the form of a truncated cone. How does this gallery function during the ignition, combustion and explosion of the rocket? No one knows. There are as many explanations as there are pyrotechnists who have studied the problem. But the fact remains: without this gallery in the form of a truncated cone in its inmost recesses, the rocket remains an inert object.'

Capolini put the cartouche back on the table and smiled at me with an air of ironic superiority.

'I have already told you,' he went on, 'that the explosion our mixtures prepare must be delayed in time and displaced in space. There's a vital word here that governs our whole profession: commemoration. Fireworks are essentially commemorative. Every country has its national holiday which commemorates an event considered symbolic, which marks a beginning. We have the storming of the Bastille, remembered every fourteenth of July, France's national holiday. But on the twenty-first of July it's the turn of Belgium, which commemorates the accession of Léopold I in 1831. The next day, the Poles celebrate the anniversary of the 1944 declaration of their independence by the

Lublin Government. On the first of August, Switzerland remembers the foundation of the Confederation in 1291. On the sixth of September, West Germany becomes one year older, because that was the day the Bundestag met for the first time in 1949. I could quote you all the national holidays in the calendar. After all, it's our daily bread! Special occasions that include firework displays are becoming much less frequent. Royal marriages these days are celebrated quietly, with a discretion that seems like a kind of shame. Ah, magnificence is not what it used to be, my dear Monsieur! People are afraid to stand out from the crowd, to be beautiful, rich, happy. The world is going into purdah . . .'

What amused me as I watched him doing his act was the total indifference of the two workmen who, apparently deaf and blind to our presence, got on with their own devices. For they seemed to be playing with their cardboard tubes, their rocket-sticks, their pots full of various-coloured powders; it was light-hearted work – in a word, fun. And anyway, isn't a firework the very symbol of useless luxury, of a fortune that goes up in smoke to provide a few minutes' pleasure?

'What about security?' I asked as we went out. 'Aren't you afraid of accidents?'

'Accidents? Never! For as long as Ruggieri's has existed, there has never been cause to deplore a single explosion here. All possible precautions have been taken. There is not the slightest flaw in our security arrangements. It would take . . . I don't know . . . an act of malevolence, a suicidal intent . . . I just can't imagine . . .'

I walked through the streets of the little town, pensive and amused. Is it true that gunpowder was invented by the Chinese but that it never occurred to them to put it to deadly use? It took the Occidentals to come up with the diabolical idea of firearms. And I remembered the monument at Freiburg im Breisgau to the German Benedictine Berthold Schwarz, who is said to have perfected gunpowder in the fourteenth century. A monk . . . a German . . . and called Black . . . wasn't it all a bit caricatural?

I would be telling a lie if I were to claim that I did a lot of work in the days that followed. The bowling alley under the plane trees that, morning and evening, drew a quarrelsome little crowd, but one fundamentally very respectful of a verbal ritual, commanded all my attention. I observed that these matches were no more open to women and children than African indabas. Isn't the game of *boules* all that remains of a sort of assembly of elders intended to reveal the soul of the community? But the heat no more encouraged me to pursue these socio-cultural reflections than to do any serious work on my manuscript. What a ridiculous idea of my publisher it had been to send me here in the middle of summer to work! My siestas lasted later and later into the afternoon, and I could see the day coming when I would have to make an effort to get up before the first game and the first apéritif. A brutal event interrupted this deplorable trend.

A venerable old man with the head of a Roman emperor was taking aim at a group of bowls bunched around the jack.

'It'll be a massacre,' muttered the man standing next to me, shaking his head gravely.

The bowl took off, described a graceful trajectory in the direction of the jack, but at the very moment when it struck the other massed bowls a noise like thunder shook the air, putting to flight hundreds of sparrows which had been dozing in the branches of the plane trees. Then, over by the Ruggieri factory, the whole sky lit up. It was once again a fireworks display, but chaotic, crazy, a blazing free-for-all in which you could catch a glimpse of cascades, Roman candles, windmills, Catherine wheels, girandoles, all jumbled up in a ghastly, infernal mess. *Hic et nunc.* I remembered Capolini's expression: an explosion here and now, neither delayed in time nor displayed in space, the catastrophe which was supposed never to happen.

People were already running in the direction of the factory. Cars stopped. Other people came out of their houses. Shopkeepers shut their shops. The village population, so accustomed to Ruggieri's fireworks that they didn't even notice the ones that went off with the loudest bangs, had immediately realized that this time it wasn't just a harmless demonstration and, as all the factory workers came from the vicinity, panic gripped the town.

I followed the general movement. The gendarmes were trying to keep the crowd out of the factory grounds. There were no more flames or fire, just clouds of acrid smoke shot through with livid reflections. Firemen were coming and going, and the people crowded round the stretchers which they were bringing out with great difficulty. I looked around for Capolini. Would he have agreed to talk to me? Wouldn't he have thought that I had been the foreign bird of ill omen for his factory? Finally I went home, driven away by the sense that I was interfering in what was none of my business.

The next day Sidonie brought me the first news. There were two dead – the two men in the workshop where the explosion had occurred. Plus a dozen wounded, one of whom was very badly burned. No one had any idea what had caused the catastrophe. As Capolini had told me, such a thing could not happen. And yet it had happened. The factory had been temporarily closed, although the damage could be repaired fairly quickly. I learned the identity of the victims: Gilles Gerbois and Ange Crevet. The first was fifty-two, the father of three children. The other was forty, and a bachelor. Both were local men. Their photos appeared on the front page of the newspapers next to that of Capolini, who kept repeating that an accident was not possible in his factory and that therefore . . . therefore . . . The only thing the reader of these confused declarations could do was examine the two faces, the one massive, obstinate, heavy-eyed, already jowly, the other intense, troubled, evasive. Did they know what had happened, or did they die unawares, astounded, not understanding a thing? I vaguely remembered Capolini's remarks during my visit. Accident impossible . . . Only an act of malevolence, a suicidal intent . . . Absurd! How was it possible to imagine a crime or a suicide in such circumstances? I went on examining the two badly-reproduced photos. I could still see the two workmen absorbed in their ridiculous devices while Capolini held forth. Even so, what an odd couple they were, that Gerbois and that Crevet! I felt an urge to go to the newspaper office and ask to see the originals of the photos.

That evening I went for an apéritif at the café in the square. The men drinking at the counter were all talking at the same time, and to the ears of a man from the North, such as myself, their provincialisms didn't make it any easier to understand what they were saying. But many of them seemed to have been personally acquainted with the two men, judging by the way they referred to them as 'le Gerbois' and 'le Crevet'. Some even said 'le petit Crevet', which conjured up a very strong image and corresponded to the thin, tormented face I remembered. 'Unlucky, no doubt about that, he never had any luck, that chap. What with all the accidents he was always having, something like this was bound to happen sooner or later.' The man who made these sweeping statements seemed to have the approval of the little group listening to him. But which one was he talking about? Gerbois or Crevet? I was dying to ask, but I didn't dare break in on the conversation, given my Parisian looks and my northern accent. As on the previous day, on the site of the accident, I felt I was being indiscreet. So I left, annoyed with myself and with the others.

The next day I questioned Sidonie about the two men. I didn't get anything very precise out of her, except that Crevet 'didn't amount to much', that he had had dozens of different jobs and that he lived alone in an old caravan just outside the town. On the other hand, she had a high regard for Gerbois, the respectable father of a family, whose wife was 'a good girl'. I could get no more out of her.

Later, walking down the street, I came upon a modest shop-window in which the pages of the *Dauphiné libéré* were displayed. It was the office of this local daily paper. I went in and introduced myself as a writer from Paris who had come to write an on-the-spot Provençal column. Almost the truth, all things considered. The Ruggieri catastrophe interested me, and in particular the personalities of its victims. The editor brought out the thick file of this very recent news item. It contained a photo of the caravan

Crevet had lived in, but he told me that it had already been removed. The said Crevet's curriculum vitae mentioned that, as the illegitimate child of a demoiselle Crevet, who died when he was only about twelve, he had been brought up, if you can call it that, in care in Avignon, not without enlivening his stay there by running away several times and being brought back *manu militari*, until the day he joined the army and was sent to Algeria. After that, more or less unskilled jobs – olive-picking, sheep-shearing, lavender-harvesting; working as a motor mechanic, builder's labourer, navvy, etc. – alternated with periods of unemployment and brief sojourns in prison for peccadillos. I made a note of the broad outlines of the fate of this humble marginal. As for Gerbois, apart from his address, I got a faint inkling of the ill luck that had dogged him – because he was obviously the one the man drinking in the bistrot had been referring to. Indeed, this placid man seemed doomed to industrial injuries. In 1955, on a building site, a load of tiles being hauled up on a crane fell off and broke his shoulder. In 1958, he was concussed when a mine exploded while the Pernes-les-Fontaines road tunnel was being bored. In 1963, he was knocked over by a runaway lorry on the hill leading out of Gordes. The following year, while the plane trees were being pruned, a chain on the saw broke, kicked back and lacerated his face. In 1967, during roadworks on the Route Nationale 542, a barrel of tar tipped over and burnt his feet. In 1970, while the vines were being sprayed with copper sulphate, he got some in his eyes. Capolini must certainly have been unaware of this series of misfortunes when he gave Gerbois a job in his factory. I thought of the famous question the highly superstitious Mazarin never failed to ask when he was thinking of giving a responsible post to a candidate who had been recommended to him: 'Is he a lucky man?'

I waited a week and then went to the address the paper had given me. Adrienne received me without too much surprise in a house where friendly chaos reigned. Since Gilles's death she had been living in an atmosphere of mourning and condolences which seemed both to have gone to her head and to have overwhelmed her. The moment I arrived she launched into a prolix eulogy of the dead man, which mainly concentrated on the years of the Occupation and the time of the Liberation. Gilles, she claimed, had been the great hero of the maquis in the Sorgue region, the leading light in the liberation and purge of August 1944. For several weeks, she said, he had reigned like a warlord over Monteux and its environs. Ah, how he had made the traitors and collaborators tremble! Adrienne was only speaking of this from hearsay, because she was born in 1940, but Gilles's heroism was inscribed in the history of Monteux. But after that, after that? What good had it all been? What had he got for his pains? Nothing, not even a medal! she lamented.

I mentioned the name of Ange Crevet. She exclaimed: 'Ange and Gilles? The best friends in the world, Monsieur. Inseparable, you might say. For young Crevet, Gilles was a big brother, a bit like the father he never had, if you see what I mean. Wherever Gilles went to work, Ange would soon turn up. They had to take him on, too. And they died together in the same accident – that was only natural, as they had always worked as a team.'

These last words surprised me. Then they had worked together before they went to Ruggieri's?

'But of course, Monsieur. As labourers on a building site, as navvies on roads being built or repaired, as pruners and farm workers when they couldn't find anything else. My goodness, when you haven't any qualifications you have to turn your hand to anything!'

Adrienne seemed to be deliberately ignoring the repeated accidents of which Gilles had been the victim. I made no mention of them.

That evening I went back to the *Dauphiné* office to get more information. Unfortunately, the editor was engrossed in a story about the difficulties that seemed to be in store for the holiday-makers returning at the end of August. For him, the Ruggieri catastrophe was settled, disposed of, relegated to the files. I must admit that I didn't really know what I was expecting from him. What still intrigued me, though, was that strange couple, those repeated accidents, and the mystery of the deadly explosion at the factory.

I hung around a little longer, and came across the first page of the first number of the *Dauphiné libéré* displayed under a glass plate: the entry into the town of the tanks of the First Army, the rejoicing crowd, the last German soldiers taken prisoner by the F.F.I. The date: 11 August 1944. 'Hm,' I thought, 'the eleventh of August was also the date of the accident at Ruggieri's.' Seeing me trying to read the leading article, the editor put in: 'Vincent Bure, who wrote that article, retired a long time ago, but he's still hale and hearty, and no one knows more about Monteux during the war and postwar years than he does. If you would like to go and consult him, I'll tell him to expect you.' I agreed enthusiastically, and after a brief telephone call it was arranged that I would call on him the next day in the late morning.

He lived near the station in a vast building which must have been a workshop or a warehouse. It was ugly and gloomy, but as spacious as anyone could wish. Bure was a jovial, shaggy bear of a man. He was very garrulous, and his accent was so colourful that there were times when I had to ask him to repeat what he had just said. He apparently had a mania for documentation. 'Luckily,' he commented, walking through rooms cluttered with files and piles of newspapers, 'there's no shortage of space here. But the most important part of my files, you know, is in here!' And he slapped his forehead with the flat of his hand. 'When I die, what a loss for local news and gossip! Ha! ha! ha!' And he laughed at the good trick he would be playing on his fellow Monteulais by dying. 'Because, you see, I was born in 1918. I'm very glad of that. Obviously I missed the 1914–18 war. Although . . . My father was in it and he never stopped talking about it. I heard so much about Verdun and the Chemin des Dames that I ended up believing I'd been there! Then, of course, there was the Popular Front, the Spanish Civil War, Hitler and Mussolini, the Phoney War, the Occupation and the Liberation – I was there all right, and even in a front seat. As a journalist, you understand! When I saw young men coming to work on the paper after that, I was so sorry for them that I laughed. Poor mutts! They arrived when it was all over. Because you must have noticed, haven't you? Nothing ever happens any more! Ever since the Liberation, it's been dead calm. Apart from Indochina and Algeria – just ripples, Monsieur, far-off ripples! And after that, nothing, absolutely nothing. They're kind enough to send me a copy of the paper. But how often in the morning, once I've glanced through it in thirty seconds, do I say to myself: "Poor mutts! But if you were honest you wouldn't have printed this paper! You'd have put a big notice up in your window: nothing has happened since yesterday, so no paper today!" Ah, you know, I'm glad to be out of it. I go back to the events I lived through. Real ones, they were! Sometimes a neighbour drops in to see me. He'll ask me: "Well? What's new?" I'll tell him: "The Sixth Army under the command of von Paulus has surrendered at Stalingrad." He'll say: "Good gracious me, you wouldn't be getting a bit cracked, would you?" Because the time before, I'd told him: "The Japanese have just sunk the American Pacific Fleet at Pearl Harbor." Or else: "The Italians have hung Mussolini's corpse on the hooks of a butcher's shop in Como." Ah, we didn't get bored in my day!'

I had a job stemming the tide of his oratory. Finally I managed to put in: 'Yes, but even at this moment there's sound and fury in Monteux. What about the Ruggieri catastrophe?' He jumped.

'Ruggieri? Now, there it's quite the opposite. Ever since I was a child I've been waiting for something to happen in that joint. I knew something was smouldering there. I told myself: "It's smouldering, it's smouldering. But when will it actually ignite?" Well, it finally ignited and blew up. But it took its time.'

'I went to see Gilles's wife and kids yesterday. Did you know him?'

'Did I know him! The leader of the F.F.I. in the Sorgue. A great fellow, he was!'

He stood up, went over to a pile of newspapers and began to scatter them around.

'Here we are, here we are. Gilles, here he is with his maquisards, being cheered by the population.'

73

He unfolded some yellowed newspapers covered in photos and headlines in enormous type.

'Here, he's pushing some German prisoners in front of him. He was the first to welcome the tanks of De Lattre de Tassigny's First Army.'

'And that? What's that?'

I put my finger on a photo of a thin, bald woman tottering barefoot in the middle of a group of laughing men.

'That? Hm, that's the shrimp, of course – la Crevette.'

'La Crevette?'

'Yes, a poor girl who lived with her kid in a hut on the outskirts of the town. She earned her living doing odd jobs, but in actual fact she used to sleep around. She was the Monteux trollop. You could say that all the men in the village had made it with her. And so naturally, when the German soldiers arrived, they had a go too. Until it became the turn of the Americans. But you know how it is. It wouldn't have been a proper Liberation without a shaven woman. And as la Crevette had slept with the Germans, Gilles and his lads went and fetched her, tied her to a chair in the marketplace and shaved her as bald as an egg. And everyone laughed and laughed . . .'

'And then?'

'Ah well, you know, if it had been up to me, we'd have let it go at that. The Liberation was a celebration, a superb celebration. A day like that shouldn't have been tarnished. Only there'd been a Resistance-fighter killed in the woods. So they got hold of la Crevette, they half-undressed her, made her take off her shoes, and then forced her to go with them to lay a bunch of flowers on the spot where he had fallen. Ah, believe me, it was a sorry procession! That pitiful, bald Crevette who had nothing on but a pink run-resistant slip, and the men laughing because they could see her black bush through it. She stumbled barefoot over the stones, sometimes she fell, Gilles booted her up, she had to go on. Personally, I was nauseated. And I wasn't the only one to think that it was easier to torment that poor girl than to fight the Germans. Only, as you can well imagine, no one dared open his mouth to protest.'

74

'What became of her afterwards?'

'She went back to her hovel and lay low. We never saw her. A few charitable souls must have taken her some food. Here, it was after the Liberation that we suffered most from hunger, you know. She sent her kid out begging and to do the shopping. And then one day, it must have been two years later, we heard that she was dead. La Crevette had never been very healthy. Her poor kid was put in the orphanage in Avignon.'

'Did you know him?'

'No, not really. He was called Ange, I believe.'

'Ange Crevet?'

'Of course, since he was the son of la Crevette.'

'But in that case, he was the one who was blown up with Gilles Gerbois?'

'Ah, that's quite possible. Hm, I'd never made the connection. But is it relevant?'

Was it relevant! On 11 August 1944, Gerbois had been la Crevette's tormentor. Ange was then ten. He lived alone with her in a hovel, and it's easy to imagine the fierce attachment there must have been between those two poor wretches. The child would no doubt have been in the front row of the spectators when Gerbois and his men had shaved la Crevette, and then undressed her and dragged her off to the grave of the maquisard. And thirty years later, again on 11 August, Gerbois and Crevet died in the same accident. One of Capolini's words came back to me now: *commemoration*. The word that governs the pyrotechnist's profession. And so far as I know, the inhabitants of Monteux do not commemorate their 1944 liberation. Except one of them, perhaps. But in that case, what a strange bird young Crevet had been, all the same!

It took me four days' research to find someone who would talk to me about him. This someone was Adèle Gerbois, Gilles's sister, an old maid and a dressmaker. I finally tracked her down in her house in a winding alley climbing up between crookbacked houses with minute gardens. The picture she painted of the relations between Gilles and Ange was altogether different from

75

the one his widow, Adrienne, had given me. What was more, the dressmaker didn't seem to think much of her sister-in-law.

'She's a good girl, and she means no harm, Monsieur, but she's of limited intelligence, and practically illiterate.'

I had immediately noticed that the walls of her little sitting-room were covered with shelves full of books.

'My brother deserved a lot of credit for marrying her. He did it because of the children. She stopped him making a success of himself as he should have.'

She was full of reticence. But she dropped her reserve when I ventured to mention Ange's name.

'I don't like to speak ill of the dead, Monsieur, but that young Crevet always worried me. It was impossible to know what he was thinking, he was always tormented, taciturn, and unstable, too, unpredictable. I never saw him laugh. A real savage, Monsieur.'

'Did he have any friends?'

'Friends? No, not so far as anyone knew. Except my brother, alas! He seemed to be pursuing him, you know. How many times did he manage to get a job with the firm he was working for! He was like a millstone round Gilles's neck. One day I asked him whether he wasn't afraid of that queer character. He gave me a peculiar answer: "I'd rather have him with me. At least I know what he's up to." You saw how it ended.'

'A woman?'

'A woman? She would have had to be quite mad to get involved with him! No, so far as we knew, he didn't have any. Except his mother, of course. Ah, you have to say that for him! He made a real cult of her. I help the verger look after the abandoned graves in the cemetery, and I can tell you that he took flowers to his mother's very regularly. He had his own calendar. A maniac for dates, he was. Although we didn't really know what they stood for. His mother's birthday, her feast-day, the date of her death, perhaps. For the rest – a mystery. But on certain fixed dates you could be sure of seeing Crevet arriving in the cemetery.'

Commemoration. Once again Capolini's key word came back to my mind. I had a sudden inspiration.

'Apropos of dates . . . Gilles had some accidents at work, I believe. Do you know exactly when?'

'You want to know the dates of his accidents? That I can't tell you exactly. You'd have to ask Adrienne. She must have that in her papers.'

Two hours later I was with Gilles's widow and I had what I was looking for. Clearly a little surprised, she nevertheless dug into some cardboard boxes full of a jumble of papers. She fished out some employment slips, reports of accidents, sickness records. It was hardly a question of being able to reconstitute Gilles's whole unlucky life. But I discovered that the chain of the saw that had slashed his face had snapped on 11 August 1964. That the lorry that had run him over had gone out of control on the hill outside Gordes on 11 August 1963. That the load of tiles had fallen on his head on 11 August 1955. Our search turned up nothing more. The simple-mindedness of this woman, who was incapable of deciphering these hieroglyphics and totally indifferent to the obsessive recurrence of this date, finally discouraged me. After all, what business was it of mine? I was neither a policeman nor a relation of Gilles Gerbois. It was only curiosity that motivated me, a curiosity that, given my profession as a writer, I might at a pinch be forgiven.

A last box contained letters, which for Adrienne were an even more incomprehensible harvest of information than the rest. Vaguely disgusted, and with an undeniably guilty conscience, I went through these vestiges of an unknown past. I was just putting everything back in place when an envelope caught my attention because of the childish hand in which the address was written. It contained a sheet torn out of a schoolboy's exercise book on which was written in clumsy letters in purely phonetic spelling:

WEN IME GRONE UP I SHAL KIL YOO
ANGE
11 orgust 1944

'What's that?' Adrienne asked me.

I put it all back.

'Nothing. Just some childishness.'

So far as I was concerned, I now knew all that mattered about this affair. True, it was still full of blanks, mysteries, ellipsis points. Yet I didn't want to know any more about that love-hate story which had ended in a firework display. It was high time for me to start my famous thriller at last: that story of an act of vengeance protracted throughout a whole lifetime, set in a little provincial town where everyone knows everything . . .

Blandine or
The Father's Visit

'We bachelors are at the same time vulnerable and threatened!'

Anselme had come out with this statement, delivered in peremptory tones, after a long silence during which he had listened to the grievances and demands of the other unmarried guests. Then he had grabbed a bottle of cider and begun to fill their glasses, as if this were a way to make sure of a quiet attentive audience.

'We complain about the demands of the tax man, who comes down heavily on the bachelor with sadistic partiality. But there is also our lack of mobility. Big firms are apt to imagine that because he has neither wife nor children to trail after him, a bachelor can be moved, transferred here, there and everywhere, to the provinces or to the ends of the earth. A traveller without luggage, he can supposedly be moved around at less cost than a married man. No doubt this is true for his employers, but for him it's a disaster. For a family man has a minimum human environment attached to him, which he can take with him. His wife and children are a little society which follows him as best it can in his migrations. The bachelor also has a human environment: his relations, his men friends, his women friends, his familiar hunting-grounds, a club, a social life. None of these things is transportable. When he's transplanted, he suffers total, profound solitude. It will take him years to reconstitute the human terrain without which he is deracinated and in a state of social deprivation.

'Yes, truly, we are vulnerable and threatened,' he repeated,

79

'and I have just experienced this in a most curious fashion.'

Then he fell silent for a moment, the better to focus our attention.

*　　*　　*

My house is close to both the church and the village primary school. One of its charms is the sound of the church bells, the other is the distant, refreshing squeals from the playground. It's a house open to all comers. That's another feature of the bachelor's life. It's the woman who shuts the doors of a house. She is the guardian of the home, an often jealous guardian, who sometimes has rather too much of a tendency to isolate her husband. We all know that: one out of every two friends who get married is a friend lost. Madame wants him to herself, and she is hostile to the complicity created by relationships dating from before her husband's marriage.

By contrast, my door is always open. Four times a day little groups of chirping schoolboys and girls pass the wide-open garden gates. Often, on a fine day, they venture into my garden. I have hazel trees, apple trees, cherry trees, a medlar. If you look carefully you can find wild strawberries at the bottom of the walls in the spring. And then there is the curiosity aroused by the peculiar trade I follow, that of photographer. How can anyone earn his living like that? Now, at least if I had a shop where I sold cameras and films, if they saw me functioning at christenings, marriages, hunts! But no, I am a 'reporter'. Actually, they don't really know what I do. And so, of course, this trade that isn't one, these open doors, the absence of a mistress of the house – all this arouses the scorn of respectable people and the curiosity of children. They risk an expedition. They meet me, we get to know one another. It doesn't take long to explore the house, and they are pleased to notice that the freezer contains a stock of ice cream. I replenish it at the same time and in the same spirit as I do the birds' feeding-trough and the cat's saucer.

I might mention that these incursions are almost always made by the little boys, even though the school is mixed. Little girls are more timid – or have been warned off – and are not so ready to venture into the house of a stranger. Incidentally, it is remarkable that in spite of all the so-called 'permissive' talk, people's attitudes – at least on this point – have remained very traditionalist. I would like sociologists to conduct a survey in the big towns, on the days when there is no school, and to count the number of boys and the number of girls roaming freely in the streets. I am sure they would find ten boys for every one girl.

A friend whom I was telling about these children's visits to my house and the rarity of little girls among them exclaimed: 'Lucky for you! Beware of little girls! Don't touch, hands off! In spite of what they say in would-be enlightened circles, you can do anything you like with the boys. The little girls are traps set to catch . . . idiots, they're trouble-makers, little horrors.'

I had only half-believed him, knowing his inveterate pessimism and misogyny. But I thought of him again on the day last summer when I made Blandine's acquaintance.

I had brought out my 5 x 4 camera with all its gadgets – tripod with focusing rack, filmpack holder, light meter, range-finder, and even electronic flash to light up the shadows in a shot taken in bright sunshine. I was trying to photograph a couple of fat bumble-bees which were fooling around noisily in the spikes of a lavender bush. This photographic record might interest a semi-scientific and very glossy magazine which pays quite well, but it required infinite patience, because it went without saying that I couldn't expect my two little creatures to show the slightest spirit of co-operation. No sooner had one of the bees appeared in my viewfinder and come into focus than it decided it was time to move on to another flower before I had managed to take the photo. I was concentrating, tense, close to exasperation, when an enormous intruder came bounding up almost between my legs, barged into my tripod and knocked my filmpack holder over. It was a big dog, rather like a sheepdog, hairy, black and jovial, which unceremoniously lifted its leg over my lavender and then got itself tangled up in my flash cable.

Immediately afterwards I heard calls, clear voices, laughter, and then two little girls came into view. I have forgotten everything about one of them, who must have been grey, or transparent, or even invisible, because I could have eyes only for the other, she was so delicate and pretty. The black cotton overalls trimmed with red braid that schoolchildren used to wear have disappeared, and I regret them. Nothing sets off the freshness and sweetness of a child better than a dark, severe garment. Above her golden thighs, Blandine was wearing a very short, light-blue smock, pulled in at the waist by a flower-bedecked belt. She burst out laughing when she saw her dog disporting himself in the middle of my equipment, and I immediately thought of one of Botticelli's angel musicians. She went charging after him and managed to grab hold of his collar, but he was heavier than she was and he sent her rolling over on the grass. I was drinking in this enchanting spectacle with my eyes, and wondering what the devil had got into me when I took it into my head to photograph bumble-bees.

We introduced ourselves. She lived with her parents, her two older brothers and her younger sister in an isolated little farm a kilometre away from the village. 'But,' she told me, 'we're going to move soon.' Her father was employed in a factory that made electrical equipment, which was at quite a distance. He left early and came home late. During the holidays they didn't go anywhere, seeing that they lived in the country.

I took them into the house and showed them my darkroom and some of my work.

'You must come back one day and I'll take both your portraits,' I promised hypocritically. 'But next time, don't bring the dog.'

For we had left him outside and, crazed with solitude, he was raising Cain in his desire to go home.

We parted. They ran off laughing, with the dog ecstatically jumping up at them from all sides, and I remained alone, dazzled and a little sad, with my 5 x 4 camera and my lavender, which the bumble-bees had finally abandoned. What can be more melancholy than a photographer who has nothing left to photograph, as he has allowed the only image that now counts for him to escape?

Blandine came back. Alone, without her companion, and in my blindness it didn't even occur to me to be surprised at this. I made a series of portraits of her which are indisputably the best thing I have done in twenty-five years of photography. I was a little worried for a moment when I suggested giving her a set for her parents and she refused: 'Oh no, they wouldn't be interested!' I didn't even dare ask her whether they knew about her visits.

One rainy day, she came in shaking the droplets off her golden hair. Then she hung up a crackling raincoat, translucent and light as a dragonfly's wing and, without waiting to be asked, headed for the kitchen. I lit a fire in the hearth. She made tea and toast. Tea for two. It was enchanting, glorious, idyllic. I kept thinking about Lewis Carroll, that clergyman-photographer who organized parties in his rooms exclusively reserved for little girls under twelve years old. He made them up, dressed them up, arranged them in groups or in tableaux vivants, and recorded on film for all eternity their ephemeral, fragile and delightful immaturity. I persuade myself that I personally heard from his lips the reply he murmured in tones of offended modesty to a friend who asked him whether all these children didn't sometimes get on his nerves: 'Be quiet; they are three-quarters of my life!' And it was his shyness that made him lie about the fourth quarter, which undoubtedly also belonged to his little girl friends.

How old could Blandine be? Eleven, perhaps – twelve at the very most. But I knew instinctively that puberty had not yet caused her blood to flow. I could see it in a hundred details that cannot mislead: a certain rather casual lack of constraint in her movements, the scars on her round, ingenuous knees, and certain gestures such as, when she was waiting or bored, putting the sole of her right foot down across the top of her left foot, a posture common to boys and girls, but typically pre-pubertal.

Oh, don't laugh! I am not so foolish as to confuse immaturity with innocence! Blandine was as artful as they come, as I was to find out from fairly bitter experience. On the contrary, I believe that, not being hampered and blinded by the ferment of sex and of the heart, the child is sometimes capable of more cunning than the adolescent wrestling with his moods. It is not rare for puberty to turn a lively, knowing child into a rather ridiculously self-conscious angel of innocence. Above all, Blandine was incredibly feminine. I have often had occasion to observe this exquisite precocity in little girls so young that they are still practically babies. Even before the age of two, some know that a man is a man and is entitled to the sort of behaviour on their part that is summed up by the one word coquetry. By comparison, little boys remain unthinking ninnies – except, of course, with regard to their mothers – until the age of their first ejaculations. Blandine had taken possession of the house, of the garden, of myself, with supreme naturalness, and I allowed myself to drift into a situation which for me was like a fairy-tale.

One day she didn't come. Nor the next day. I waited for her the whole week, eating my heart out. But at least I could hear the squeals from the school playground, and I persuaded myself that her voice was among them. The weekend was all the more lugubrious in that the weather was glorious. On the Monday I committed the stupid blunder I had been trying to forbid myself all week: I went and waited for the children to come out of school, thus exposing myself to the comments of the whole commune.

She came straight up to me and said simply: 'Papa wants to see you.'

This was the threat that had been hanging over us ever since our first meeting, and that I ought to have averted by taking the initiative, and that no doubt I would have averted had Blandine not inexplicably thwarted all my vague impulses to visit her family.

'Whenever he likes. What time does he want to come and see me?'

'He gets home from work at seven.'

'Tomorrow, half past seven.'

'I'll tell him.'

And she walked off, very upright, very serious, with nothing of the playful grace she usually displayed with me, in my house. It was quite clear that from now on the ghost of the father was watching over her and surrounding her with an atmosphere of disapproving authority.

From that moment I began to wait. Whatever I was doing – an order for five hundred colour prints demanded all my time, if not all my attention – amounted to no more than an anxiously impatient way of filling in the time. Being the way I am, waiting for certain things fills my life to the exclusion of all activity, of all thoughts that would be foreign to them; they are truly tyrannical periods of waiting. This noble, avenging father – what accusations could he throw in my face? Feverishly, I kept re-examining my memories of every one of Blandine's visits, of the hours we had spent together, and in all honesty I could find nothing very culpable. But Blandine was at the delightfully uncertain age when tenderness is confused with desire, and the friendly pat on the back with the amorous embrace. How ready people are to treat us bachelors as seducers, whereas more often than not we are simply the seduced, the prey and not the hunters, the victims and not the torturers!

The doorbell rang. It was he. If I had expected a wrathful, stiff-backed, majestic patriarch, I had been very much mistaken. He was a small man with a pale, sad face under a beret pulled right down to his ears. A workman's shoulder-bag – for his lunch, no doubt – completed his working-class image.

He sat down on the edge of a chair.

'Blandine told me you wanted to speak to me,' he began.

This lie with which the interview started increased my feeling of unease, all the more so as I had no way of telling whether it came from Blandine or from her father. Nevertheless, it would do as an opening gambit, and I accepted it at once.

'Of course, of course. She comes to see me quite often. And it's only natural that I should want to introduce myself to her parents.'

I asked him what I could offer him. He finally accepted a glass of beer. No, thank you, he didn't smoke. A vast silence fell. It was incredible how little we had to say to each other! I observed him incredulously, repeating to myself without being able to believe it: 'This is Blandine's father. She owes him her life. He sees her and kisses her every day.' How bizarre the natural order sometimes is! For his part, he looked around with curiosity.

'Blandine has told me a lot about your house,' he said.

The rather painful idea flashed through my head that in fact, while Blandine might be slightly attached to me, it was certainly less for myself than for this house in which she reigned supreme, and which obviously must have made a change for her from the family home. I stood up, and offered to show him round. This might contribute to winning each other's trust. Ground floor. Living room, where we were now. Study. Kitchen. Cloakroom. Door opening on to the staircase leading down to the cellar. On the first floor, the bathroom and four bedrooms. But the most important area was on the floor above, the converted loft, panelled with narrow pine planks. This was my photographic studio. And this was also where I had put my bed, because I like to sleep among my spots, my trays, my tripods and my cameras. As a schoolboy, when I went to bed I used to take the textbook for the next day's lesson for which I was the least well-prepared and put it under my pillow. I believed that while I was asleep the text, being so close to my head, would come and imprint itself there by a kind of telepathy. It is no doubt by virtue of a similar belief that I like to sleep within the shadow of the instruments to which I owe my living and my freedom.

'It's big,' Blandine's father commented.

Big? Obviously, a house in the country is always more spacious than a town flat. But, I told him, I was 'big' enough myself with my professional activities to fill all this space.

'Even so, it's big,' he insisted.

Then, quite naturally, he went on to talk about his own housing problems. No doubt Blandine had told me. They were soon going to have to move. The little farm they had occupied for eleven years – well yes, actually since Blandine was born! – was being reclaimed by their landlord, who, to make quite sure of getting rid of them, had found them a place they could move to some thirty kilometres away. One of those mass-produced developments where all the houses were the same and faced each other across a rectangular lawn no bigger than a rug.

'So the thing is,' he concluded, 'I came to ask you whether you might know of anything in the neighbourhood. You never know, something might crop up, even a rather dilapidated house which I would take it upon myself to repair. I'm not fussy.'

I promised, touched by this appeal for help, turning over in my mind the people I knew, but it was obvious that in this part of the countryside overrun with secondary residences there is less and less room for people of modest means. I promised to ask around, yes, but my tone of voice showed clearly enough that I didn't have much hope.

Neither did he, for that matter, but that wasn't what he wanted from me. For his grey face unexpectedly lit up with a smile and, as if in the grip of a sudden inspiration, he raised his hand towards the staircase.

'But you here! You're not short of space! Since you're always up on the second floor in your loft, why shouldn't you rent us the first floor?'

This sudden proposition caught me unprepared. It took my breath away. And he lost no time in insisting, as if my staggered silence were an initial sign of agreement.

'We wouldn't be a nuisance, you know – me, my wife, the four kids and Pipo.'

'Pipo?'

'Yes, that's the dog.'

Hm, I'd forgotten the dog, but then I called to mind that big affectionate brute knocking my filmpacks over and lifting his leg over my lavender.

I finally managed to pull myself together. No, really, it was impossible. It couldn't be considered. I was less on my own than I seemed. Friends came to visit me. And family, too. The rest of the time, my work called for peace and quiet. And the layout of this house – the way all the space was in its height – made isolation impossible. The moment there was someone in one of the bedrooms, I could sense him, even if he was a model of unobtrusiveness.

I spoke in this vein for a long time, gently, but allowing a definitive refusal of his crazy proposal to filter through my words.

His smile faded only slowly, as he lowered his eyes to the bottom of his glass in which he was automatically rotating the remains of his beer.

'It's a pity,' he murmured, 'it's a pity, it's a great pity.'

Then, suddenly, he looked at me. The lower part of his face was still vaguely smiling, but his little grey eyes were staring at me with chilly animosity.

'Yes, it's a great pity. Because if we don't find anything, well, we'll have to go, won't we? And Blandine, well, she'll go too!'

African Adventures

Do you know Ceuta? It's a strange little port on the Moroccan coast facing the rock of Gibraltar, which is the European Pillar of Hercules. The African Pillar of Hercules is Mount Hacho, just outside Ceuta on the tongue of the peninsula. To the west, then, the Ocean; to the east, the Mediterranean; to the north, Spain; to the south, Morocco. As for the town itself, it is a Spanish enclave on Moroccan territory, administered from Cadiz . . . It's all quite bewildering. The population of Ceuta is mainly Spanish Catholic, although naturally there are also many Berber and Arab elements.

I was staying in a charming villa which a friend had lent me while he was on a trip to Europe with his wife. That's the sort of invitation I appreciate. Why do people always want to make us the prisoners of their own presence? I like them to invite me, yes, but after that I like them to be tactful enough to disappear and leave me sole master of my surroundings!

My room opened on to a covered veranda facing the Mediterranean east. The first rays of the rising sun, skimming over the crest of the waves, came to rest in a golden patch above my head. The first sea breeze was suffused with the fragrance of lemon trees and magnolias, for there was a medium-sized garden between the house and the line of rocks against which the waves broke. In short, I need say no more; you have, I think, grasped that I was in paradise.

My solitude was not total, for my friend had left me his servant Mustafa, a grey-haired Muslim with a grave, gentle smile. He arrived before dawn, saw to the house and the flowers, made my lunch, and left at noon.

One day I was awoken by voices coming up from the garden, which mingled with the babbling of a sprinkler and the peaceful sound of a rake being drawn over the sandy paths. I took a few steps in the garden, then sat down to drink my tea. A boy of about twelve was collecting the rare dead leaves that had fallen on to the sand, stopping every so often to move the sprinkler. I exchanged a few words with him. Later I asked Mustafa who he was.

'He's my youngest son, Hatem,' he answered promptly. 'I don't know what to do with him now that he's left school. He helps me with odd jobs. Youth unemployment is our national scourge.'

'He's very good-looking,' I said casually.

Good-looking he certainly was, blond and blue-eyed as the Berbers of this region often are, but the only expression on his perfectly regular features was a rather obstinate solemnity which cast a shadow over his childish face, whereas the same gravity on his father's face was informed with intelligence and acuity.

I had got into the habit of going up to my room after I had drunk my tea, lying down again and reading or writing in bed for an hour or two. A few divine moments went by. The sprinkler went on gurgling, but I couldn't hear the rake any more. There was a scratching sound on my door. Then it was pushed open. It was Hatem. He hesitated. I told him to shut the door. He could have taken that to mean that I was sending him away. But no; he entered, shut the door behind him, and came and stood in front of my bed. A faint smile lit up his melancholy face, just as a ray of sunlight sometimes shines through the rain. I threw back the bedcover a little and said: 'Get in!' His few clothes fell to the ground and he slid in beside me. I squeezed his little buttocks in my hand; they were hard and contracted, like two apples, the buttocks of one of those boys with principles who abominate sodomy.

'Aren't you afraid your father will come up?' I asked him after a moment.

He shook his head.

'Does he know you're here?'

A nod.

'Did he send you?'

He nodded again. I kissed him, and thanked God that such a beautiful country should also be inhabited by men who were so good and so intelligent.

The next morning I had confirmation from Mustafa himself of the accuracy of what Hatem had told me about his father's sentiments.

'Hatem, you know,' he told me when he brought me my toast, 'he's very fond of you. You ought to take him to France with you. He'd be useful to you. He can do everything: cooking, cleaning, gardening. And with you, he'd learn to read and write.'

I was comforted by the obvious wisdom of this father. He knew that nothing could better help his son make his way in life than a European protector to whom he would be attached by a physical relationship. Marvellous Islam, so far removed from the stupid antisexual fanaticism of our Western society!

Unfortunately, though, Mustafa's proposition could not have come at a worse time – in more cruelly ironic circumstances, I mean. A week earlier, coming back from Marrakesh, I had found myself in a precisely similar situation, and I had had such a slap in the face that I was still reeling from it. It happened at Chichaoua with a boy a little younger than Hatem, who was called Abdullah.

Ah, that boy! he can boast of having charmed me in every sense of the word. I had barely stopped in the main square of Chichaoua, a mountain hamlet clinging to the flank of Djebel ech-Chaoua, when he unceremoniously slid into my car and assured me with a big laugh that I couldn't do without a guide to visit the Medina, to buy sheepskins, and to discover the Andalusian garden. Did I need a room? Yes, I answered, but in an hotel where they don't ask for your passport, because I wanted to share my room with a Moroccan friend. Highly intrigued, he suddenly became serious and asked me where my friend was. 'Beside me in the car,' I answered. He couldn't stop laughing, and there is no doubt that it was for his laugh that I loved him, just as one loves the sun for the warmth and light it spreads over everything. Abdullah was as dark and gay as Hatem was blond and melancholy.

We went and bathed in the Ras el Ma cascade, which was horribly cold. Abdullah's body was smooth, round and hard, like one of the pebbles on which the water comes crashing down. Then he took me to a house in the Medina which gave no sign of being an inn, where we had a twin-bedded room of memorable filth. But Abdullah was so beautiful and so engaging that everything around him turned to gold, alabaster and carved ivory. I was awoken in the middle of the night by the violence of my happiness, and I woke him to tell him that I was going to take him to France, that he would be my companion for ever, that I was offering him my life. Then I went back to sleep, with the feeling that I had settled an issue that was immense and definitive.

The next day, when I opened my eyes in that frightful hovel, he had disappeared, taking with him all the cash contained in my pockets. I had offered him my life, and he had preferred six hundred and forty-five dirhams. Such *disinterestedness* caused me a kind of bewilderment close to nausea.

Hatem and Abdullah, Abdullah and Hatem . . . what tricks love and chance played on me that Moroccan autumn!

Lucie or
The Woman without a Shadow

I shall call her Lucie. She was my mistress and I loved her. I was, to be precise, ten years old. I shall never forget her multi-coloured woollen dresses or her long, black, full gypsy skirts, her scarves, her shell necklaces, her ballet slippers (I never saw her wearing that abomination, high-heeled shoes!) Under the raised table, on a level with our faces, her bare, tanned legs would be wrapped round each other like a thick coil of flesh, soft and flawless. Above all, I shall never forget the crown of wild flowers she wore one Midsummer's Eve when she danced round the bonfire with us. She had a plait which she either wound round her head or left hanging down her back. Because I had an illustrated album of Slav folk-tales, I thought she looked Russian or Ukrainian; exotic, in any case.

You may not quite have understood me when I spoke of my mistress. It is indeed most remarkable that we use the same word to designate a married man's lover, his second woman as it were, and the teacher in charge of the youngest schoolchildren. For it should be remembered that we French speak of a '*professeur*' for the older ones. A child's first woman is obviously his mother. The teacher he finds at school is the second woman in his life, his mistress, and not infrequently he inadvertently calls her Maman. Is that such a crime? One may wonder. In the old days the schoolmistress was traditionally an ugly old maid with a pince-nez and her hair scraped back in a bun, a caricature figure of the dried-up old hag. I am quite prepared to dispute this image, but my Lucie's story may perhaps prove that it was wise to guard against any sort of confusion.

I was ten years old, then, and I loved my mistress. I was prepared to get up to any sort of trick to be in her good graces. As I was a mediocre pupil, neither brilliant nor a dunce, not remarkable for anything whatsoever, this was no easy task. Especially as my passion was shared by every pupil in the class. Everything conspired to convince us that we were creatures apart – privileged, prestigious – because we belonged to Lucie. I tried Sophie. She was a classmate. She was also Lucie's oldest child; Lucie had two younger sons, Tibo and Tijoli. Only it seemed that a wall had been erected between Lucie-mistress and Lucie-mother, because Sophie took visible pains not to give any indication of being related to her 'mistress', and like the rest of us she never addressed her as anything other than 'Madame'.

For a long time I was obsessed with the idea of walking Sophie home after school in order to witness Lucie's metamorphosis, when she could once again be called 'Maman' by her daughter. It seemed to me that the said metamorphosis would be valid for me too, and would enable me to cross the threshold of a well-defended intimacy which I imagined to be paradisal. Yet although I had twice had the chance to go to the former level-crossing keeper's house where Lucie and her family lived, and although I had been able to catch a glimpse of the glaucous, vegetal canvases that her husband painted, I had waited in vain for Sophie to pronounce the magic word, the veritable 'Open Sesame' of that family. It took a catastrophe for its doors to be opened to me.

But I must say something about my own family, which formed the other pole of my juvenile life – alas, a negative pole. Money. I believe that a man's relations with money are every bit as profound and complex as those he may have with God, his own body, his wife, his mother, etc. My father earned a lot of money. No doubt that perpetually-replenished flow of money was as indispensable to his mental health as the oxygen he breathed was to his physical survival. How does one make a fortune? The answer is simple. All you have to do is, from childhood, to think of nothing but money. Actually, 'think' isn't the right word. It requires both more than that, and less. Without ever having formulated to himself any kind of strategy for his life, the future multimillionaire automatically orients all his thoughts and all his actions towards a single goal: profit. This is an integrated reflex, and so deep-rooted that it always remains subconscious. Naturally, this fundamental orientation has an origin which can sometimes be determined. With my father – and no doubt his is a fairly common case – I think it was the mental wound that the lack of money had inflicted on him and, worse than that, the humiliating spectacle of his parents squabbling over an empty purse. Like many others, this had marked him for life. His hatred of the degrading poverty he had experienced in his childhood turned him into the formidable business tycoon he later became.

I must also specify the nature of his business, for it played a part in my story. My father's first job was with a local, 'peripheral' radio station, which was the term in those days. Peripheral meant commercial, for at that time the national radio's sole source of income was the tax paid by listeners. He was promoted, and then became the commercial director of a rival station, after which he founded his own advertising agency. The advertising profession is no doubt one of the most elegant and rapid ways to make a fortune. To seduce the crowds by incorporating the product to be sold into the image of a paradisal life whose ingredients are carefully-measured doses of happiness, beauty, youth, eroticism, holidays . . . To seduce! My father had perfectly adapted his conduct and states of mind to this end. His motto could have been: seduce or die. But I don't think he would have been able to achieve so much in his profession if his nature had not been so well suited to it. He was the perfect example of the type described in characterology as 'Venusian'. For him, flattering appearances took the place of morals, and when reality intervened and upset, or even destroyed, this beautiful façade, all that remained to him was hatred. I can imagine, and not without pain, the surprise of a girl intoxicated by the charms of this prince of appearances and the day after a dream marriage discovering the other side of the picture. It seemed as if my father, weighed down by the remorse caused him by the lies invented by his business, justified himself in his own eyes not only by an excess of professional gravity, but also by an austerity in his private life which his wife and son were naturally expected to share. My mother and I were subjected to a régime whose contrast with the life-style simultaneously surrounding us bordered on the absurd. We had a car and a chauffeur at our permanent disposal, but we were only allowed pâtisseries for dessert at Sunday lunch. Any waste – but particularly wasted food – and a drama would ensue. Twice every winter we went skiing in Gstaad, but our shopping had to be done in the nearby supermarket. Our house had a servants' wing where a cook and a housemaid lived, but I never saw an expensive perfume on my mother's dressing table. For a long time I believed that she fully shared her husband's taste for this curious mixture of luxury and austerity, and if I had been more mature I would have thought of her family's Calvinist origins, the branch of Protestantism that produced Puritanism and the millionaire ascetics of American capitalism. She didn't seem to suffer from her submission to the style – so peculiar, so constrictive – of her husband. Never a scene, never a tear. With hindsight, I think she was living in a state of extinction. The parental bedroom constituted a sanctuary in the house I knew I was not allowed to penetrate. How did I know this? This taboo must have been inculcated in me so young that I respected it as a natural law.

Yes, she lived in a state of extinction in that funny sort of family which was not at all a funny family, in which any emotional demonstration, any remotely lively expression of feeling would have been considered a breach of good manners. And one day she must have emerged from this torpor, and she left . . . I have never been able to decide the proportions of grief, humiliation and fear of scandal in my father's reaction. If I hint that genuine grief played very little part in it, I shall be accused of anti-paternal bias. I heard of my mother's departure from the servants. When I went in to dinner, only two places were laid. My father drew me towards him, placed his hand on my head and said in a solemn voice: 'My son, your mother has abandoned you.' This turn of phrase surprised me, because I had rather thought that it was him she had abandoned. But no doubt those simple words – 'My wife has abandoned me' – would not have been able to shape themselves in his mouth. I was deeply hurt. The silence in which this meal took place was abominable. Not only had my father not known how to make my mother happy, but he was also proving to be just as incapable of carrying on any sort of conversation with me. That evening I measured the emotional desert I was living in. I went to my room, taking the apple I had for my dessert. A splendid summer was coming to a close. Night was falling gently over the still gardens. Maman had gone. And I? What was I doing there? My room was on the ground floor. I jumped out, and, apple in hand, I started down the road leading to Lucie's house.

I was expecting to find in contrast a house full of lights, music and scents. I was surprised to find it dark and silent. I went up to the door but, even before I had raised my hand to the bell, it opened of its own accord. Lucie was there, standing in the semi-darkness in which her nightdress appeared as a big, whitish patch. One detail struck me immediately, and I thought it of marvellous importance: her plait was undone, and her shoulders were covered in a cascade of dark hair. Not knowing what to do, or what to say, I held out my apple to her, and she accepted it. I managed to get out: 'Maman has gone.' She said: 'Come in!' and led me into the house. 'Nicolas has taken the children to his mother's. They'll be back tomorrow morning. Have you eaten?' I wasn't hungry. I was carried away by this miracle: Lucie all to myself! Not only the class but her own family had disappeared and left us alone together. But wasn't my mother's flight in itself the necessary prelude to this enormous bliss?

And night fell. My recollection of the hours that followed is vivid but vague. It was so long ago! And then very obviously I slept. At the age of ten one has no gift for staying awake. Night. Why has no one yet expressed all that night permits? Permission, submission, remission, admission. Night is the total abolition of prohibitions and sanctions. It is collusive silence, contact, but also transgression. If thefts, crimes, gaming, escapes, prostitution choose the night, it is not only because the darkness makes surveillance more difficult, it is also because night is by nature the time of anarchy. I lived that anarchy in Lucie's arms in a state of bliss I have never recaptured. Since then I have never stopped pondering on the mystery of that great illumination. I believe I was drinking at the very source of the milk of human kindness that Lucie contrived to distribute to the whole class through her lessons and her presence. But above all it was a nocturnal milk, and Lucie owed her radiance to none other than the shadow that she knew how to preserve in herself.

My upbringing had no more accustomed me to lie in in the morning than it had to sit up late at night. The dawn was only just breaking when I opened my eyes. Lucie's big brown body, lying across the bed, enveloped me in an archipelago of dishevelled hair, abandoned hands, massive thighs, and breasts with big, blackish-brown lunules. The contrast between her sleep and my wakefulness made me feel uncomfortable. The companion who is asleep is blind to her companion whose eyes are open, and cruelly eludes him. She takes refuge in an inaccessible world and casts him out into the harsh, exterior brightness. I slid out of the bed. I was just going to leave the nuptial chamber after one last look at my sleeping mistress, when I noticed a doll on the floor at the foot of the bed; I must have knocked it out as I got up. I picked it up and put it back by Lucie's side. If I remember rightly, it was one of those curiously composite dolls of a past era, because its china head was hard, round and brightly coloured, while its body, made of some padded fabric, was soft, swollen, shapeless, and of a greyish colour. I had time to see its eyelids droop over its blue glass eyes as it resumed its horizontal position by Lucie, one of whose hands dreamily came to rest on it.

I wandered for a while through the deserted house. It was in such chaos that I couldn't have said which was the kitchen, the dining room, the living room, the library. There were books, food, games, garden tools all over the place. What a contrast with the obsessive tidiness of my family's house! How I would have loved to live amongst this friendly bric-à-brac! But the major revelation was Nicolas's studio, a sort of glass cage, more precisely a veranda stuck on to the house. Because its walls were entirely concealed by huge canvases, the light came from above. But is that the way to describe it? In actual fact each canvas radiated its own light, but naturally this wasn't the flat, realistic brightness that came through the glass roof, it was a rich, complex light, at once disquieting and alluring. The colour that dominated Nicolas's paintings was a special sort of green, not chlorophyllian but aquatic, salty, exactly what they call *South Seas blue*. And yet the alarm was raised at the same time by the touches of pink that evoked mucosae, viscera, wounds. No, it wasn't an innocently vegetal green but the fundamental hue of the life that comes from marine waters and which is just as much putrefaction as germination. We learn from mythology that Chronos, having cut off the genitals of his father, Uranus, with a sickle, threw the lot over the balcony of heaven. The sickle became the island of Malta. The genitals floated for a long time at the mercy of the waves, surrounded by a pink, brackish foam; they were finally cast up on a shore as a bloodstained medusa, from which emerged a woman of incomparable beauty, called Aphrodite (*aphros* = foam), and later identified with the Venus of the Latins. It was this panting, fecund flesh, heavy with Venus-like ravishment, cradled by the eddying currents, that Nicolas tirelessly represented on his canvases. Femininity itself, nascent, and therefore charged with all its original force. I dimly understood that it was a ten-times-repeated portrait-in-depth of Lucie, for I had just emerged from her arms and was still completely impregnated with her emanations.

The irruption of Nicolas and the three children put a sudden end to my investigations. I could hear them causing pandemonium in Lucie's bedroom. Her laughter was mingled with Tibo and Tijoli's shouts, and for the first time an unknown name reached my ears: Olga. Had she slept well? Had she had her breakfast? Was she coming for a walk with them? I was intrigued by this Olga, whose presence I hadn't noticed. As for my own presence, they seemed unaware of it. But then Nicolas came upon me in the studio. 'Ah, you're here?' Did he mean: here in the studio, or here in the house? 'What do you think of my paintings?' I should have been quite incapable of saying anything about them. 'They're all here. I've never sold a single one. They all belong to Lucie. I paint for her.' He walked round and round, flinging his arms out to right and left. He had a short fringe beard and was wearing a brown corduroy jacket and trousers. Apart from the floppy bow tie, which he was not wearing, he looked like the typical romantic artist of the past. I understood that in spite of my age he was treating me as a privileged visitor because, as he had told me, no one but his family ever saw his work. I was the only outside witness. He stopped in front of a big composition. Glaucous swirls encircled the little figure of a child, or more precisely of a doll. 'That's Olga. It's Lucie's life revolving round Olga.' I recognized the doll I had slept with in Lucie's bed, and now I knew who Olga was. 'It's a pond emptying,' I said by way of comment. I did indeed think I could see a mass of water, abounding in duckweed, algae and frog spawn, swirling around a drainage hole over which the doll Olga had come to rest. Nicolas seemed surprised. 'Ah, you think it's emptying? But if it were turning in the other direction it would be filling up, wouldn't it? Personally, I saw Olga as a source of life and plenitude. But you – you read the opposite. Well, well . . .' He gave me a perplexed, sorrowful look. 'I may be wrong,' I said, wanting to be conciliatory. 'No, that's just it, you can't be wrong. Anyone who looks at a painting can't be wrong. What he sees is an infallible truth. It's like Olga. Is she a millstone round Lucie's neck? Some people say so. Personally I think the opposite: she's the warm, colourful centre of Lucie's life. How can we know the truth? Lucie refuses to say a word on the subject.'

I didn't understand very much of this speech and I was relieved when the brothers came bursting in and exclaimed loudly when they saw me. They whisked me into the main room where Lucie was sitting at the table with Sophie in front of bowls of chocolate and slices of bread, butter and jam. Nicolas joined us. I sat down with them. What was most striking at first was the sloppiness, not to say filth, of the table and the whole house. The oilcloth was strewn with crusts of bread and bits of cake, studded with pools of milk and jam, and Tijoli's hamster was casually strolling over it, sticking its nose into the bowls and pots. Everyone was talking and exclaiming at the same time, all except Lucie, who only came out with rare monosyllables and who was devoting herself to the doll, Olga, sitting by her on the edge of the table. And yet she wasn't isolated, far from it! You felt that she was the centre of this house, that the whole house and the four other members of the family, plus the cats, the hamster etc., were all no more than something emanating from her. We were all her children, including Nicolas of course, the failed painter who had never sold a canvas because he only painted for her (and anyway, who else would have been interested in these immense, moist, moiré, musty surfaces, quivering with marshy life?)

I had my share of chocolate and brioche, and then the boys took me outside. Their knowledge of the surroundings and my inferiority as a visiting stranger made up for my being some years older than them. I have already mentioned that the family lived in a former level-crossing keeper's house. The line from Beaune to Arnay-le-Duc which crossed the road almost at a right angle had not been in use since well before I was born. The rails and sleepers had been removed. The sleepers were piled up not far from the house. When Nicolas had the energy to saw up some of them – the century-old wood was hard enough to put anyone off – they burnt them in the fireplace in the house or the stove at school. At school we used to protest because of the smell of creosote that filled the classroom, which was the same as that of the latrines in the playground. The old railway embankment had become a strange path of stony soil where hemlock and wild sorrel flourished. It was impossible to cycle on it, and even walking was difficult. And yet we all dreamed of a particular expedition to a terrifying and mysterious place of which the 'big boys' spoke in glowing terms: less than two kilometres away was the big black mouth of a tunnel, ready to swallow up the candidate for initiation. That was where the two brothers, taking advantage of the unexpected support of an older boy, had decided to go that morning. They triumphantly showed me the candles and matches they had provided themselves with. We had to leave at once.

Their excitement lent them wings, and I had difficulty in keeping up with them on the broken stone ballast as they went dashing down it. A strange track, perfectly level but rough, where for a century locomotives had hurtled along before plunging into the mouth of the tunnel, shrieking like mad things. Stripped of its rails and sleepers, it had something of the look of a sorrowful, nostalgic Way of the Cross, punctuated by signal-posts which still displayed their discs and their mutilated semaphore arms. When the entrance to the tunnel finally came into view round a bend, I felt I was approaching the gate to the beyond. But the time for hesitation had passed. 'What are we going to look for in there?' My question was lost in the enthusiasm of the two brothers. The entrance was inadequately closed by a few bits of barbed wire and a board with these words scrawled on it: NO ENTRY DANGER. But Tibo and Tijoli had already disappeared.

The ground seemed strangely soft and elastic after the sharp stones of the ballast. We were walking on brushwood, faggots actually, laid down to form a continuous carpeting. The air was motionless, cold, humid, and anyway, when we stopped and listened, we could hear a distant trickling sound. The brothers had each lit a candle and were moving forward, holding them above their heads. But the light they gave was pathetic, and the increasing darkness soon brought us to a halt. Looking back, we could see the entrance to the tunnel, a luminous orifice in the shape of a vault. 'We ought to be able to see the exit soon,' said Tibo, 'the tunnel is in a straight line, I know.' We took a few more steps, but the complete darkness stopped us once again. Tibo gave his candle to his brother. 'I'm going to collect some wood and make a torch.' The murmur of the stream became louder, the humidity of the air increased, bathing us in a soothing coolness. I felt marvellously far away from my family, from school, from all the vicissitudes that made me so unhappy. 'It must be like this when you're dead,' I thought. There was a crackling sound and a sudden flash. Tibo was brandishing a big bunch of lighted brushwood. 'Let's go!' We continued our advance. The ground was now sloping very gently downwards. The vault over our heads was shiny with humidity. Something white brushed against our heads and disappeared. 'An angel,' Tijoli suggested. But we had to stop again, and this time for good. The vault had collapsed, and now formed a confused mass of rocks and earth in front of us, over which a torrent was pouring. 'The spring must have undermined the tunnel,' Tibo observed judiciously. Tijoli knelt down and plunged his hands into the bubbling water. Then, half-turning, he sprayed us with it. The torch went out. My face was dripping. We instinctively turned round towards our point of departure, a tiny prick of light piercing an ocean of darkness. 'This time we're going back,' I said. But suddenly my heart missed a beat. The luminous aperture was turning red, at the same time as an acrid smell reached us. 'The faggots! We've set fire to the faggots! Quick, let's get out of here!' I took the two brothers by the hand and made a dash for it. The ground was fairly slippery, but the main thing was that the smoke was getting thicker as we advanced. I knew we would have a carpet of fire to break through. Everything depended on how wide it was. Tibo and I were wearing strong shoes, but Tijoli was barefoot in light sandals. We could no longer see each other when he called out to me that he'd hurt himself. I picked him up in my arms and went on, afraid now that I might fall over. The carpet of fire appeared. Judging by the proximity of the entrance to the tunnel, it wasn't more than about thirty metres. I rushed on, followed by Tibo. We burst out into the sunlight in a torrent of smoke, like the young Hebrews Shadrach, Meshach and Abed-nego coming forth unharmed from the burning fiery furnace at Nebuchadnezzar's command.

It wasn't Nebuchadnezzar who greeted us but the three village gendarmes, attracted by the smoke they had seen billowing up from the forbidden tunnel. They had also been informed by my father of my disappearance. We were covered in soot and besmeared with tears. We turned to look at the shadowy mouth vomiting clouds shot through with purple flames. It was barely believable that we had come out of that hell intact! And then there was a fantastic apparition which has marked my life for all time. At the heart of the black and gold conflagration a big white bird was thrashing about. It was the owl that had brushed against us earlier. For a moment it beat its wings on the spot, like some diabolical golden oriole, and then, having cleared the tunnel, it soared up, passed over our heads, and disappeared into the foliage. We had time to see its flat face and rounded eyes turned in our direction. And so, because of our misdeeds, the bird of Minerva, instead of taking flight at twilight, as the philosopher has it, had been torn from its sweet familiar shadows and was escaping desperately into the midday sun.

The sequel is sad and can be told in few words. Escorted by the law, we went back to Lucie's house, where the two brothers disappeared. As for me, I was taken home to my father. Today I realize how devastating my flight, after that of my mother, must have been to him. He reacted with unqualified brutality. I learned that I was going to be taken by night under close guard to Cahors, where I was to be a boarder with the Jesuits. I only heard much later how he had taken his revenge on my mother and Lucie. Where Lucie was concerned, he had quite simply lodged a complaint for corruption of a minor. The fact that she was a teacher made her offence much more heinous under Article 333 of the Penal Code. As for my mother, I was to have no more news of her for the next seven years. My father himself gave me the reason for her silence during an argument we had when I was fifteen. There had been a divorce in which my mother was declared the guilty party. Nevertheless, my father gave her a comfortable allowance – thanks to which she was able to keep her lover – but only on condition that she would break off all relations with me. The merest visit, the merest letter, and the monthly payments would cease. She respected the contract scrupulously and my appeals were met by total silence. You have to have some knowledge of an adolescent's sensitivity to be able to gauge the contempt and hatred that such a situation inspired in me both for my father and for my mother. Ah, how they had betrayed me, how they had conspired to cause my unhappiness! I only became free of these feelings when I was twenty-three, on the day I met the woman who was to become my life companion.

But two years before that, I had had the curiosity to enquire about Lucie's fate. On a passing visit to my father's manor house, I had gone for a walk down the disused railway track. A family I didn't know was living in the level-crossing keeper's house. A yellow dog rushed up to me, barking. I hadn't the heart to go on as far as the entrance to the tunnel. But I met the postman, and he told me that Lucie's family had gone their separate ways, judging by the different addresses to which he forwarded the letters of its five members. He gave me the addresses of Lucie and Nicolas. Lucie was the head of the girls' lycée in Beaune. Nicolas was working in an industrial design studio in Dijon. Apparently they were separated.

I had phoned the Beaune lycée to say I was coming. She received me in her office in a manner that was both sprightly and serious, which she must have perfected for the parents of her pupils. Where was the generous soul of my childhood, the inspired slut of the level-crossing keeper's house, the archipelago of breasts, stomach and thighs in which I had known bliss one night when I was ten years old? Lucie had become perfect, impeccable, polished. Her hair drawn back, her make-up matt, her eyes oblong and dry, a little, round, white batiste-collar over a severe, grey, elegantly-cut dress, she looked like a de luxe nun. I scrutinized her passionately, trying to find in this varnished mannequin the warm woman I had loved.

Inevitably she brought up the past, a long period of trial and error, according to her. She had been possessed by ghosts that had almost destroyed her. Fortunately an admirable doctor – more a confessor than a physician, to tell the truth – had made her see herself clearly. A catharsis, a purge of everything in her that was turbid and impure, had made her into a new woman, transparent, efficient, healthy. After a two-year break she had gone back to teaching. But on a higher level. There was now no question of her 'taking a class'. What is a class? A big animal with thirty heads and sixty feet. A monster that moves, giggles, fidgets, whispers, scratches, falls asleep, dreams. And on top of that, artful, unpredictable, sensitive to the seasons, to storms, to the dog days, to the frost. The teacher feels enveloped by this monster, sometimes bogged down in a soft jelly, sometimes attacked on all sides as if in an acid bath, or at other times hypnotized by a look shot from the depths of this amorphous mass, which he finds impossible to meet. For a long time corporal punishment constituted the normal physical contact between the student body and the teaching body. A fair, logical contact, but at the same time overflowing with sado-masochistic overtones. It used to be the indispensable safety valve of a far too human relationship that cannot be resolved by purely verbal exchanges. It is no longer the fashion, and while some parents do not hesitate to come and advise the teacher to thrash their offspring if necessary, while some children, vaguely aware of an incomplete relationship with their master, solicit a liberating hiding by their attitude, the master for his part must be able to resist these tempting but dangerous demands.

The truth is that teaching is inexorably evolving towards impersonality. And this is logical. Because there's a complete break for the child between his family and school. School is not a big family. The family, as a biological milieu, responds to emotional currents, to the forces of passion. There, inequality, promiscuity, the whims of feelings hold sway. We sometimes try to control this anarchy. Good table manners, the formality that rules in certain households, the prohibition of incest, that taboo of taboos (although so frequently flouted amidst general silence) are so many attempts to introduce a little taming into the family menagerie. The problem is particularly acute when the mother of a family is also a teacher and has one of her children in her class.

This was what had happened to her with her daughter, Sophie, and she had done her best to get her to observe the difference between the 'Maman' at home and the 'Madame' at school. Because true order is only to be found at school. Only at school does justice prevail. All schoolchildren are equal before the school's rules and regulations. The only things that count are work and discipline. A child who is unhappy in his family will say: 'They don't love me.' A rebellious schoolchild exclaims: 'It isn't fair!' And often this is the same child, and he has perfectly understood the difference.

I listened to Lucie's calm, objective, transparent exposition. And I looked at her, a woman of glass, transparent herself, cold and colourless. Ah, how well that guru of hers had washed her, rinsed her, spin-dried her! How had she come to this? And where was she going? She answered this second question in concluding her speech. The normal culmination of modern teaching, she told me, is the computer, the robot-teacher devoid of every trace of emotion and therefore infinitely patient and objective, taking into account all the particularities of the single pupil placed before it, both his shortcomings and his aptitudes, and distilling into him at an appropriate pace the information in the syllabus. She was working towards this ideal . . .

My head was spinning somewhat when I came out of this interview. I repeated the question to myself: how had she come to this? And the other mysteries that surrounded her: what had happened to the family after I was sent away to school at Cahors? Why had she separated from Nicolas? Obviously he was the person I now hoped would be able to throw some light on the matter. A few days later I phoned him at the industrial design studio where he was a draughtsman. He told me that he couldn't say when he would be free to meet me, but that he would call me back as soon as he had a moment. He wrote down my address. Two weeks later I had a letter from him which in fact answered all my questions. My heart had turned to ice when Lucie had insisted on calling me *vous*. But I was immediately reassured by the warm familiarity of his letter.

My dear Ambroise,

So you are now emerging from that terrible adventure in which we were all engulfed together. I gather from our brief telephone conversation that you don't know much of what happened to us, because your father went to great pains to isolate you from your former environment, and I'm quite sure your visit to Lucie won't have enlightened you. But you know that your father lodged a complaint against her for corruption of a minor. Your naïve account of the night you spent in her arms weighed heavily in the evidence against her. Well, yes, what do you expect! Naturally the whole business had to be dramatized by bringing sex into it. So there was our Lucie, suspended by the Dijon educational authority, and threatened with being taken to court, going to prison, and goodness knows what else. The children, our friends, and I myself would have laughed at such idiocy if we hadn't seen that Lucie was succumbing to a depression which frightened us. No, she wasn't taking these things lightly! She didn't speak, didn't eat, didn't move. She stayed for days on end with staring eyes, hugging Olga in her arms (Olga, you may remember, was her fetish-doll). It was as if in the shipwreck of her life that doll was her sole lifebuoy. This went on. Interminably, for us. There was no option but to put her in the hands of a doctor. Some trick cyclist or other. He came, he tried to get her to talk to him, but she refused. It was agreed that she would go and see him twice a week. Before he left, he said: 'That doll is the key to the problem.' In spite of my prejudice against him, I was impressed. That was what I had always suspected. So I agreed to take Lucie to see him regularly in Beaune. He kept her for about an hour, and then I brought her home. By force of circumstance, then, I followed the effects of this psychotherapy step by step. I watched Lucie gradually emerge from her mutism, and at first this was a great joy. The dead woman was returning to life. In the meantime the Dijon authorities approached your father, he withdrew his charge, and the court dismissed the case against her. Everything seemed to be returning to normal. But that was when I became aware of Lucie's metamorphosis, which at first surprised me, but later reduced me to despair. There is no point in my describing to you the new Lucie, whom from week to week I saw coming into existence under my very eyes. You have seen the end result for yourself. One day, on our way back from Beaune, she said: 'We'll stop at the house and then go on to Commarin.' I obeyed without asking for an explanation. She went in, and came out again immediately. She was carrying a closed wicker basket and a spade. You can imagine my perplexity. So we went up to Commarin, which, as you probably know, is the village where she was born. As the car turned into the village street, she said: 'Left, for the cemetery.' We stopped the car outside the gate. We went in and she headed for a grave. To my amazement I read on the headstone: Lucie M. The name of my wife, who was right there by my side! Also inlaid in the marble, there was a photo of a little girl who could have been Lucie at the age of eight or nine. With her spade, she began to attack the grassy rectangle at the bottom of the grave, intended for flowers, although there were none. She dug a little hole. Then she opened the basket and took Olga out. The key to the problem, the shrink had said. There was also a white silk shawl. She wrapped the doll in it as if in a shroud, and laid it in the grave. Finally she put the soil back and carefully smoothed its surface. It was over. Lucie had just buried Lucie's beloved doll at the foot of Lucie's grave. I was at my wits' end. We left in silence but Lucie, who was no doubt grateful to me for my discreet docility, consented to give me a few explanations. This allowed me to ask her more questions later, with circumspection, and I was finally able to reconstitute the whole of her secret history, a history of which I, her husband, had been totally ignorant.

She was the only child of a couple of small shopkeepers. Her parents had inherited the Commarin drapery. I *couldn't say why, but it seems to me that the cosy, frugal atmosphere of that particular trade was rather in keeping with the covert, morbid, sanctimonious behaviour of her parents. Lucie must have been about nine when by chance she discovered a grave in the village cemetery that bore her surname, her Christian name and her photo. It was a terrible shock, but she didn't breathe a word of it to her parents. She had absolutely no doubt: she was dead and buried and, like ghosts in fairy stories, condemned to carry on the pseudo-existence of phantoms on earth. 'It wasn't always unpleasant,' she told me. 'I felt light, irresponsible, entitled not to take anything or anyone completely seriously.' She lived in a sort of funereal intoxication, which she fostered by making regular visits to the cemetery to lay flowers on her own grave.*

This lasted for two or three years, but one day reality brutally obtruded itself. Up in the attic there was a big old-fashioned trunk, which was locked. Lucie managed to get hold of the key, and she explored the contents of the trunk. Inside was the past, all the vestiges and souvenirs of Lucie, another Lucie, clothes, toys, a doll (Olga), and a big photograph album. There was a bundle of papers containing prescriptions, a burial certificate and a funeral notice, from which it became apparent that she had died at the age of nine from cerebro-spinal meningitis. It was clear that her parents had hidden there everything that might remind them of that first daughter, gone never to return, to make room for the other Lucie, the replacement, the double, conceived and born in the same year as the death of her sister, my Lucie, our Lucie.

So now you know what Olga was, and why Lucie took her down to her room and never stopped taking care of her, cherishing her. She was at the same time her dead sister, imprisoned by death in eternal childhood, and her own double. The attention she lavished on her was aimed at warding off and taming the shadow that opened up beneath her, with every step she took. It was an admirable formula, and for ten years it filled the level-crossing keeper's house with colourful, voluble happiness. Admirable, fecund, but fragile. It was like an audacious, graceful, magic scaffolding, but it was unstable, and all the more threatened in that it was erected on the frontiers between a clear conscience and an obscure heart.

I was the first to benefit from it. I was a second-rate draughtsman. Lucie made me into the painter whose works you saw. Perhaps posterity will discover them one day, long after I am dead. In actual fact, all I did was reproduce the colours that emanated from Lucie. Iridescence. I registered this word in particular when I heard it used by chance. From a Greek word meaning rainbow. A property of certain bodies that enables them to produce the colours of the rainbow. Where did Lucie get this gift of iridescence? I have no hesitation in replying: from the shadow that was in her, that other Lucie, dead and become Olga, the doll with the sleeping eyes. But once again the construction was fragile. It was a miracle that it held up as long as it did. Lucie deployed her iridescence over her schoolchildren like a gentle fan. She didn't play the educationist's game. Too much complicity with the girls, too much of a mother with the little boys, too much of a woman with the bigger ones. It couldn't last. And there were her own children, the critical eye of Sophie, a little rival provoked by puberty in the face of her mother, the increasingly outrageous antics that Tibo, imitated in everything by Tijoli, got up to (the fire in the tunnel was only one of their many excesses). And I, the failed painter, living off his wife ... Don't accuse yourself unjustly. Your running away and your father's brutality brought down an edifice that was already tottering. The shrink gave it the coup de grâce. From his first intervention, I stopped painting. What would I have painted from then on? The iridescence was extinguished. I went back to the drawings of my youth, that's to say in black and white. These days I *draw engine parts. Can you imagine anything further removed from my feverish salt marshes and paludal mucosae? But perhaps that is my own way of remaining faithful to Lucie, of coming to terms with the new Lucie? I too have chosen light with neither shadow nor colour. That's the point we have all reached now, and you will always remain a privileged person in my eyes because for a moment you shared our long walk in the holy shadow of the forest of Brocéliande. It has closed behind us, leaving us alone in the harshness of broad daylight. We must learn how to turn the page. We must be strong to be able to go on living.*

Nicolas

Turn the page. Leave behind us the holy shadow in which we had walked. That I refuse, with all my strength. I have locked that shadow into my heart for all time, and the baptism Tijoli administered to me in the depths of the tunnel with his nocturnal water has marked me for ever. My symbol will remain the white bird of Minerva suddenly appearing in the blazing sunlight from a burning, roaring cloud.

To Write Standing Up

The Cléricourt prison visitor had warned me: 'They have all committed serious offences: terrorism, hostage-taking, hold-ups. But outside their hours in the carpentry workshop they have read some of your books, and they would like to talk about them with you.' So I had taken my courage in both hands and set off for this descent into hell. It was not the first time I had been to prison. As a writer, of course, and to talk with those particularly attentive readers, young prisoners. I still carried with me the unbearable aftertaste of these visits. In particular I remembered one splendid June day. After two hours of conversation with human beings similar to myself, I had left in my car, saying to myself: 'And now they are being taken back to their cells, and you are going to dine in your garden with a woman friend. Why?'

They confiscated my papers, and presented me with a big, numbered token in exchange. They ran a metal detector over my clothes. Then some electrically-controlled gates opened and shut behind me. I went through a series of closed doors. I walked down corridors that smelled of polish. I climbed staircases protected by netting. 'To prevent suicide attempts,' the prison officer explained.

They were gathered in the chapel, some of them very young indeed. Yes, they had read some of my books. They had heard me on the radio. 'We work in wood,' one of them told me, 'and we would like to know how a book is made.' I spoke of my preliminary research, my travels, and then the long months of solitary craftsmanship at my table (manuscript = hand-written.) A book is made like a piece of furniture, by the patient adjustment of its various bits and pieces. It takes time and trouble.

'Yes, but a table, a chair – we know what use they are. A writer – is he useful?'

The question had to be asked. I told them that society is threatened with death by the forces of law and order weighing down on it. All power – political, police, or administrative – is conservative. If there is nothing to counterbalance it, it will create a closed society, like a beehive, an ant hill, a termitary. There will be nothing human any more – in other words, unexpected, creative. The writer's natural function is, by his books, to kindle the fires of reflection, of contestation, of challenge of the established order. Tirelessly he calls for revolt, for disorder, because there is nothing human without creation, yet all creation is disturbing. That is why the writer is so often harassed and persecuted. And I cited François Villon, more often in prison than free; Germaine de Staël, defying Napoleonic power and refusing to write the single submissive phrase that would have won her the favour of the tyrant; and Victor Hugo, exiled on his island for twenty years. And Jules Vallès, and Solzhenitsyn, and many others.

'You must write standing up, never on your knees. Life is a work that must always be done standing up,' I ended by saying.

One of them gestured with his chin towards the thin red ribbon in my buttonhole.

'And that? Isn't that submission?'

The Legion of Honour? As I see it, it rewards the peaceful citizen who pays his taxes and doesn't disturb his neighbours. But my books – they defy any reward, and any law. And I quoted one of Erik Satie's sayings. That poor, obscure musician detested the vainglorious Maurice Ravel, whom he accused of having stolen his place in the sun. One day Satie was amazed to hear that Ravel had been offered the cross of the Legion of Honour, but had refused it. 'He refuses the Legion of Honour,' he said, 'but his entire work accepts it.' Which was very unfair. Yet I believe that an artist can accept every sort of honour for himself, providing that his work refuses them.

We parted. They promised to write to me. I didn't believe it. I was wrong. They did better. Three months later, a van from the Cléricourt prison drew up outside my house. Its back doors were opened and a heavy, solid-oak desk was brought out, one of those tall pieces of furniture on which notaries' clerks used to write, as did Balzac, Victor Hugo, Alexandre Dumas. It had only just left the workshop, and still had a pleasant smell of wood-shavings and wax. A brief message accompanied it. 'For you to write standing up. From the Cléricourt prisoners.'

The Phantom Car

On my way back from Gascony, I had turned on to the A10 autoroute at Orléans. I soon noticed a parking area with a restaurant and service station. The restaurant was inside a covered bridge spanning the autoroute. So I drove to the foot of the bridge and found a place to park my car by a smart yellow stall in which a young woman, in a dress and cap that were also yellow, was grilling and serving aggressive-smelling merguez sausages on cardboard plates. I got out of my car and hesitated for a moment. Merguez or not merguez? Finally the smell put me off and I started up the stairway to the bridge. I found the self-service restaurant, a news-stand, the lavatories – everything to make a person happy. I ate, drank, browsed for quite a while. Then I went down the stairway again, ready to leave. The yellow stall was still there, and also the attendant, dressed in the same yellow, with her sausages . . . but no car. Disappeared, flown, my beautiful automobile! I had a shock, and then a doubt. Had I really left it there? So I went wandering up and down the rows of parked cars, searching for mine. Not there. It was a catastrophe. I had left my luggage in it, my papers, everything, everything, everything . . . What was I to do? I went back to the yellow stall, rattling my useless keys, my face registering all the vexation of the human condition. The young woman with the sausages called out to me:

'Are you looking for your car?'

'Yes. Did you see it being stolen?'

'No, but I know where it is.'

'You know where it is?'

'Yes. On the other side of the autoroute. You came from the provinces and you're going to Paris?'

'Yes.'

'You're on the Paris-provinces side. Go back over the stairway.'

I thanked her as if she were restoring my life, and rushed over the bridge. On the other side, at the foot of the stairway, I found a yellow stall in which a young woman in a yellow dress and cap was frying merguez. But my car was there, faithful and somnolent.

You look at yourself in a mirror. You are calm, everything is as it should be, your tie, your parting, your smile. But suddenly your smile disappears. Because you have just noticed a bizarre, abnormal, disturbing, monstrous detail: the wrist-watch you wear on your left wrist, yes, it's there all right, and the watch is going. Not in the mirror, though. The man reflected in it is indisputably you. But he hasn't got a wrist-watch.

I also remembered a legend. Vampires are people like you and me. Only, if you stand beside one in front of a mirror, you will see yourself in it. But the vampire won't be reflected there.

My car is a vampire-car. On the other side of the mirror there is still the stairway, the merguez stall and the young woman in the yellow dress and cap, as in reality. But no car . . .

Dangerous Pity

How can anyone be a doctor? How can anyone care profession-
ally for sick, wounded, dying people every day without being
oppressed by the morbid emanations they give out? How can he
defend himself against the contagion of misfortune?

Many years ago – I was living in Germany – this question
arose for me in the form of a tragic destiny. *Multiple Sklerose*.
These two curiously French-sounding words had been spoken in
connection with a doctor who specialized in this inexorable
disease. Actually, the doctor was only the husband. We were
going to see and hear his wife, a friend of the pianist friend I was
with. She had been his rival at the conservatoire and had given
signs of being exceptionally gifted. Then she had abandoned her
career as a virtuoso and got married. That at least was what I
understood at first.

The doctor was much older than his wife. This was apparent
more in his stooping figure than in his face, a face that still
possessed a kind of adolescent freshness, a fragile, even wounded
face. He made a contrast with his young wife, who radiated
health, brio, love of life. She went to the piano and gave us a
recital of unforgettable ardour.

'What a magnificent couple, what happiness they radiate,
each according to his own vocation!' I exclaimed, when I was
alone with my friend again later.

He smiled sadly, and disabused me. Happiness perhaps, but
of a somewhat exceptional kind, more a tragic sort of happiness!
The girl had had to give up her career as a virtuoso, with a broken
heart, when she experienced the first trouble with her eyes and
sense of balance that presaged multiple sclerosis. The doctor

who was treating her hadn't been able to bear the sight of this superb artist condemned to sink slowly into an incurable decline. Married and a father, he had abandoned his wife and children to devote himself entirely to her. Not being able to do anything for her as a doctor, he had married her, and no longer left her for a single hour. He even said he had decided to follow her into death.

How can anyone be a doctor? Precisely: some people cannot. The protective varnish with which the good, detached practitioner covers himself in order to resist demoralization, cracks under a shock that is too brutal. And the disease insinuates itself. Dangerous pity invades him like a devastating passion.

Passion, patient, passive, pathological, pathetic. Five words whose common etymology sometimes manifests itself cruelly in the facts.

The Beggar Reaching
for the Stars

It was . . . I don't remember. A few years ago. With India, you always lose track. A country that destroys everything. Faces, bodies, birds, memories, the calendar. Karl and I had decided to abandon Europe when winter was at its gloomiest and to go East. *Ex oriente lux!*

Stopover in Tehran: darkness and fog. Arrival in New Delhi: cold and wind. Short flight towards the south: Calcutta. A heat which at first seemed gentle and welcoming. We hadn't yet discovered the bodies. Normally, the Indian has no body. He is a painted face, with luminous eyes, consumed with spirituality, which proffers itself to you above a dummy dressed in rags. Nothing discourages physical contact, caresses, and especially erotic exchanges, so much as this lightweight doll which, although clothed, is none the less devoid of mystery. No, nothing either attracts or excites in the emaciated body of the Indian, who himself seems to be without desire.

And then there is the dampness. How can one covet the body of another when one is already exasperated by the weight, the humidity, the stickiness of one's own body? Indeed, India is a land of chastity . . .

And yet in Calcutta the bodies are there, everywhere, haunting you, standing, squatting, but for the most part lying all over the place. As a third of the population is homeless, they sleep at night where they live in the daytime, in the place where they work or beg. The driver sleeps in his taxi, the liftman in his lift, the costermonger on his barrow, the butcher on his slab. In the morning, they wash and do their business in all innocence in the gutter. The absence of eroticism is counterbalanced, as is very often the case, by an inordinate scatological presence.

From the very first day we had been confronted with the problem of the beggars. How could we give them nothing? But how could we give them anything without provoking a riot? For the Indian beggar no sooner receives a gift than he alerts his colleagues in a praiseworthy but catastrophic spirit of solidarity. And then the unfortunate donor is mobbed. 'I have just done a bad deed,' Anatole France wrote, 'I gave alms to a pauper.'

Karl had recourse to a stratagem at first. In the plane we had been given meal-boxes containing the elements of a modest snack. I had one of these boxes in my travelling bag and we had had the idea of letting it benefit one of the half-starved children who appeared in front of us like ghosts. But at some distance from our hotel, and wrapped securely enough to give us time to disappear. The experiment had been conclusive. Intrigued, the child had squatted on his heels and set about opening the parcel enveloped in sticky tape. He was still working at it when we made our escape.

From then on we spent part of our days buying small items of food, wrapping them up, and then distributing them at random during our walks.

The system worked for three days. The catastrophe occurred on the fourth. We could see them as soon as it was dawn from our windows. Dozens of children were keeping a lookout in front of the hotel, at a respectful distance from the doormen. The Indian bush telephone had done its work. We had been spotted. We had to go out through a back door, and of course empty-handed, which didn't spare us an imploring, tireless escort. Oh, those frightful gestures, a fist waved in front of an open mouth (food!, food!), or a little shirt pulled up to reveal a skeletal torso, or a baby held out at arm's length by a tiny little girl! What was to be done, yes, what was to be done with the beggars of Calcutta! And the most horrible thing of all was that you finally grew so accustomed to this lamentable chorus that you met with an impassive brow the fulminating curses of a ragged prophet furious at being ignored, or the red betel-nut juice spat out in disdain.

One evening the hotel dining-room had a surprise in store for us. Garlands of multicoloured fairy lights hung between the capitals of the columns and the tablecloths were decorated with sprigs of fir, which were totally exotic in this latitude. We questioned the waiter. '*Christmas, sir, Weihnachten meine Herren, Noël . . .*' he told us, imitating a delighted provincial. And my goodness, yes! We hadn't noticed the approach of 24 December, and my word, it was that very evening! These Indians couldn't have been more considerate towards the western barbarians that we were.

But Karl seemed preoccupied.

'What are you thinking about?'

'About the Howrah Bridge.'

It is true that it had made an unforgettable impression on us, that gigantic metal bridge spanning the Hooghly. Its immense superstructure was covered with a human ant hill, a compact mass of pedestrians, bicycles, cycle-rickshaws, cows and horses, in the midst of which several hundred lorries and cars seemed to be stuck for ever.

'I made enquiries. The tremendous amount of traffic is partly due to the big railway station near it on the right bank.'

'I am especially thinking about what we saw under the bridge,' said Karl.

This was the result of a rather 'Parisian' reflex I had once had. I had lived for years on the Ile Saint-Louis. I had got into the habit of making little nocturnal excursions along the banks of the Seine to fraternize with the tramp population which at that time used to find shelter under the bridges Marie, Louis-Philippe and de la Tournelle. As we drifted with the tide, carried along by the crowd on the Howrah Bridge, I had said to Karl:

'And underneath? Let's go and look underneath!'

It had been no easy task to find the alley winding its way among the hovels down to the river bank. Only the slope and the moistness of the ground gave us any sign that the river was not far away. Enormous rats scurried away from our feet. We trod on soft things which we preferred not to identify. We skirted primitive huts, low black tents, raised boards strewn with bodies shrouded from head to foot, as in a morgue. Occasionally a crazed face would loom up in front of us and then immediately disappear. A gnarled hand on the end of a skeletal arm would reach out. Some red, acrid smoke made us cough and our eyes water. Because night was falling, and as the temperature had dropped a few degrees, the Indians were huddling up in ragged groups around little fires fuelled with paper, fabrics, peelings, dung, unmentionable things.

'How many are there?' Karl murmured.

A vain question. It was more than a camp, it was a subterranean town, swarming under the swarm on the bridge, like an ant hill under an ant hill. Upstream, on the same bank, we could see the funeral pyres of Nimtala Ghat. Luckily, we passed relatively unnoticed.

'That's because we have nothing to give them,' Karl had said.

Having indeed learned from experience, we had embarked on this expedition with empty pockets, and it almost looked as if the wretched crowd knew it. In this connection, I recalled a memorable passage in Lanza del Vasto's book, *Return to the Source*. One day he went bathing and left his clothes on the bank. When he came out, he saw that the knotted handkerchief in which he had tied the small amount of money he was travelling with had disappeared. He panicked: there he was, alone, destitute, in the heart of the Indian continent! Then he burst out laughing. He had just realized that he was living through one of those rare moments when God makes it his business to give us proof that he is our only support. From then on, and for ever after, his life changed. Mysteriously informed of his absolute poverty, not only did the Indians stop begging from him and trying to exploit and rob him, but on the contrary they took him into their houses, clothed him and fed him. Nevermore would he possess anything at all. And I had copied out these words of Lanza del Vasto, which are like a precept for gentleness and trust: 'The man who falls into the waters of destitution has only to relax and wear a beatific smile. And then he will float . . .'

It was this population camping under the gigantic bridge, then, that Karl suddenly alluded to in that four-star hotel dining-room, lit up for Christmas Eve.

'What of it? What does that great bridge inspire in you?'

'Why don't we go back there?'

'This evening, in the dark?'

'Yes. We'll celebrate Christmas with them! We'll buy everything we can, and invite them to carouse with us!'

That was Karl all over, a dangerous but admirable companion, who on a sudden impulse would place you in a terrifying dilemma: either to launch out on a superb but desperate venture, or to go to earth, with shame in your heart.

'We'll go, since you're so keen,' I sighed, 'but at least let's finish our dinner first.'

It was soon disposed of. And then we went out. Nothing could have been more funereal than all those bodies on the pavements wrapped in white cloths that looked like shrouds. But in Calcutta life never stops, and it wasn't difficult for us to fill the Moses basket which had been our first purchase. Karl seemed to be carried away by the joy of the Christmas spirit. He bought great quantities of dates, bananas, sultanas, cashew nuts, ground-rice balls, mangos, pineapples, and even some of those golden fritters dripping with clear honey. He added, as a challenge no doubt, a whole lot of Indian quids, an inflammatory mixture of tobacco, betel-nut and quicklime enveloped in a betel leaf. In the meantime we were approaching the great bridge over the Hooghly River.

The crowds were as dense as in broad daylight, and it was a job, complicated by the Moses basket, which we were each carrying by one handle, to squeeze our way through the strolling throng. But the shadows, here and there broken by torches and lanterns, the silence mysteriously enveloping these mechanic-ally-moving men and women with their lifeless faces, had something unreal about it.

'Dead people,' Karl murmured. 'They are like dead people walking towards the beyond.'

'Charon couldn't cope any more and he retired,' I said. 'So they threw a stone and steel bridge over the Styx.'

A tall old man with a fierce gaze passed us without seeing us. He had a formidable, yellow-eyed mastiff on a leash.

'Rhadamanthus with Cerberus,' said Karl. 'This really is the descent into Hades!'

Do you remember in the Odyssey? Ulysses wants to consult the prophet Tiresias, who has been dead for some time. He makes his way along the banks of the River of Ocean until he reaches the cave that is the gaping mouth of Hades. On the threshold of this fatal gate he digs a trench about a cubit long and a cubit in breadth, around which he pours libations of mingled milk and honey, then of sweet wine, over all of which he finally sprinkles some white barley. The dead still don't appear. Then Ulysses sacrifices a white lamb and a jet-black sheep, and their dark blood pours steaming into the trench. And now the bloodless souls of the dead, thirsting after life, come towards the mouth of the cave. At first Ulysses guards the trench, sword in hand. A strange combat! The grey, diaphanous army of the defunct laying siege to this bloody hole, and Ulysses standing alone, repelling their assault with the point of his sword! Because Tiresias alone has the right to approach, and to quench his vampire's thirst. What Ulysses had not foreseen was the appearance of his own mother, Anticlea. He had left her full of life in Ithaca, and he found her shade among the innumerable defunct. He did not know that she had died of grief while waiting for him. He weeps, but he has the strength to repulse her too. Only Tiresias will drink the blood.

Ulysses, braving the onrush of the shades, was us, thrusting our way through that obscure mass to reach the camp of the dead. But we wouldn't have to repel them with the point of a sword, we would throw them armfuls of Christmas provender, strange Western Father Christmases, lost in these Asian confines. But we had yet to get there . . .

When we had worked our way round the last pier of the bridge, we still had to get down to the bank, and we cursed our lack of foresight because a pocket torch would have been invaluable in the muddy labyrinth in which we were feeling our way. The latest issue of the *Telegraph*, the Calcutta English-language newspaper, a copy of which was covering our Moses basket, served to light our way. Page by page, Karl transformed it into torches which, brandished at arm's length, must have made us a strange sight. Our anxiety inspired us with familiar references, which we clung to.

'Rembrandt, *The Night Watch*,' I murmured.

'Don Juan and Leporello on their way to picnic in the cemetery with the statue of the Commander,' Karl amended.

But he let out an oath, because he had suddenly slipped and fallen. He stood up, groaning.

'At least the picnic is intact. But something is intriguing me. Ever since we left the bridge, we haven't seen a living soul. The other day it was swarming around here, wasn't it?'

I didn't say anything. I too had been struck by the absence of any human beings. But it was very different when we finally got down to the bank. The starry sky was completely cut off by the blackness of the superstructure of the bridge. We couldn't see anything of the crowd moving over it in both directions, but we could hear their ant-like tread. As for the enormous area stretching out underneath the bridge and beyond it, this was deserted. The tramps' village we had discovered there, those low tents, those bodies stretched out on boards, those little groups huddled together round a smoky fire – they had all disappeared.

'Good God – but where are they?'

'They've all gone off to celebrate Christmas, why not!'

'What fools we look, with all this food!'

'What shall we do? All the same, we aren't going to take it back to the hotel!'

'Let's do what they're doing: celebrate Christmas!'

He had sat down on a worm-eaten log cast up by the river, and he put the Moses basket down between his feet. I sat down beside him. He peeled a banana.

'What admirable irony! We arrive with our hands full, fearing a furious onslaught, and here we are, our marvellous presents left on those same hands!'

'It goes even further than you think. You remember the Chaplin film, *The Gold Rush*? The unlucky little emigrant is in love. It's Christmas Eve. He invites his beloved and her lovely girlfriends to have supper with him. He ruins himself buying delicacies and little presents. He has prepared a magnificent table in his hovel, with candles on a white tablecloth. And no one comes. He falls asleep with his head on the table.'

'Yes, I remember. He dreams. He dreams that the lovely girls have come, and to amuse them he does the famous dance on the table with the French loaves.'

'The recalcitrant guests. The rich man whose presents nobody wants. The terrible solitude of the rich man. The poor huddle up together round their miserable pittance. They keep each other warm. The rich man is cold and has no appetite, alone in front of his overladen table.'

'That's the theme of one of the parables in the Gospels, the strangest and most cruel of stories. A rich man wants to entertain his best friends magnificently. He sends out his invitations and prepares the finest and most succulent banquet imaginable. On the appointed evening everything is ready. The table is resplendent with embroidered linen and gold table-ware. Nothing is missing but the guests. The host waits. The hours pass. Not a soul. So he sends his servants to find out what has happened to them. Later, they come back, one after the other, with excuses. One of the guests has bought a piece of ground, he has to go and see it; another says he has bought five yoke of oxen and has to try them, a third is getting married. Then the angry master of the house says to his servants: "Go out quickly into the streets and lanes of the city, and bring in hither the poor, and the maimed, and the halt, and the blind." The servants do so. But there is still room, and this is where we come to the sublime folly. The master says to the servants: "Arm yourselves, go out again and bring in all the passers-by you meet, with your swords at their backs if need be!" No painter has so far had the audacity to depict this incredible banquet: the sumptuous table, the master consumed with vexation and rancour, and a motley crew of cripples and unfortunates, and finally the poor passers-by, bewildered and terrified, who have been dragged there by force. No novelist has related the sequel to that astounding evening!'

There was a silence, and all we could hear then was the tread of the innumerable footsteps going by over our heads. I had said 'astounding evening' when I was speaking of a parable in the Gospels. But who would be willing to believe our Christmas evening in Calcutta?

It was hot. We may perhaps have slept a little. Later, Karl told me of one of his recent memories.

'I didn't mention it before. Yesterday morning, when I went back to the hotel on my own, a boy was doing my room. I was disturbing him in his work, and he disturbed me too. After a moment he came up and touched my shirt. I immediately told him in my pidgin Anglo-Hindi that I would give him my laundry later. He shook his head, smiling. It was a misunderstanding. He wanted something else. He took hold of my shirt between his thumb and index finger, and held his other hand over his chest. It was clear: he wanted my shirt. As a present, that is! I laughed. It was a bit much, don't you think? But I was disarmed, and gave in. So I found myself stripped to the waist, and off he went, bubbling over with thanks and with my sweat-drenched shirt. I thought of Saint Martin of Tours. That soldier was canonized for cutting his cloak in two with his sword in order to share it with a pauper. *I* had just given away the whole of my shirt.'

'But you had a dozen more in your suitcase.'

'That's true,' he conceded, starting on a pineapple.

Another silence. Sound of footsteps.

'Begging. I'm trying to understand the relationship it establishes between two human beings,' I said. 'The other day I was pestered by a young boy who was as handsome as a god. He didn't look at all wretched. Laughing, I refused to give him anything. In the end he laughed too, and his demands became more and more familiar until they seemed to be a kind of game. I went on walking, and then we got lost in the Botanical Gardens in the middle of the forest of the famous 200-year-old banyan tree's self-propagating roots. Emboldened by my obvious goodwill, he was just about to search my pockets. I stopped and looked at him. I said to myself: 'A young Arab would already have had his pants down ten times! But everything about his behaviour discouraged the slightest sexual advance. Yes, the young poor of India are cloaked in a mantle of innocence. You can't touch the Untouchables, not because of their impurity but on the contrary because of their purity. There is an absolute incompatibility between begging and prostitution. The prostitutes in the red-light districts of Bombay are superbly dressed, their hair is impeccable, and they move around in what look like theatre sets.'

'Of course,' said Karl. 'Prostitution presupposes that the prostitute is desired by the client. It is her professional duty to be beautiful, seductive, provocative. This relationship also exists in a certain sense in begging. But in that case it is you who without realizing it are handsome, seductive and provocative in the eyes of the beggar. The money or the shirt you give to the beggar is a piece of yourself or of your universe that you are delivering up to his concupiscence. The rich man is the poor man's whore.'

Silence fell again on this excellent pronouncement. How long did we remain there, prostrated by the sticky atmosphere of humid heat? At last we roused ourselves. The shimmering surface of the river was glowing with phosphorescence. We went back one last time to the black mass of the bridge weighing down on us. We left our Moses basket, still three-quarters full, at the foot of one of its pillars. And that was when we discovered him, our one and only beggar of this Calcutta Christmas. He was perched on top of the pillar. Squatting twenty metres above the ground, a great, scrawny, featherless bird, his elbow resting on his knee, in an immemorial gesture he was reaching out his open hand to the scintillating, starry sky.

A Baby in the Straw

To start with, you must imagine a tricolour flag caressed by the nocturnal breeze and set ablaze by a floodlight. Then, as the frame widens, the façade of the Elysée Palace appears, harshly outlined by the artificial lighting. A single window is lit up. Zoom in to the window. A dissolve gives you the illusion of entering the room. The smiling President of the Republic is sitting in an armchair by a fire in which flames are dancing.

'*Français, Françaises,*' he says, 'our schoolchildren have been on holiday since this morning. The end-of-year celebrations are illuminating the streets of our towns and villages. In a few days' time it will be Christmas, and then a week later New Year's Eve. It is the custom on this occasion for the President of the Republic to offer his greetings to his compatriots. I shall not fail to do so. This year, however, my greetings will be of a very special nature. This is because I wish to address you on a serious and important subject, and to make you a revolutionary proposal. Revolutionary, yes, strange as that may seem, coming from a President of the Republic, and just before Christmas, what is more. This is what I have in mind.

'When people speak of the great scourges from which our society suffers, they mention drugs, violence, tobacco, alcohol and road accidents. The figures we are given are appalling, and we must certainly fight relentlessly to reduce them. However, these scourges, thank God, concern only a minority amongst us. But there is another, more insidious, more surreptitious scourge, which is likely to lead the entire population to the most hideous degeneracy. This scourge does not even have a name. We might call it medicomania, clinicomania, pharmacomania, and goodness knows what else. But its name is unimportant. It is the figures that count, and these figures infinitely exceed those of the victims of the other scourges. One can measure evils according to different criteria. I will simply say this: every year our spending on illnesses increases faster, much faster, than the country's resources. Where are we heading? Well, it is simple, and it is terrible! An elementary calculation enables us by extrapolation to determine the precise year, month and day when the totality of the nation's resources will be absorbed by medical care. What our life will then be like is barely imaginable. Suffice it for me to say that we shall then nourish ourselves only with medicines. We shall travel only by ambulance. We shall dress only in bandages. A grotesque, infernal picture.

'What can we do to prevent things coming to such a pass? I appealed to the leading lights of the medical profession. I begged the academies to study the problem and suggest a solution. To no avail. The evil must be attacked at its root. But where is that root? What is it, then, that turns every one of us into at least a virtual invalid, forever dosing himself for a real or imaginary illness?

'Then I turned to my last resort. I remembered the village of my childhood, and the doctor who treated us – my brothers, my sisters and myself. And when I say he treated us . . . He intervened as little as possible, knowing very well that it is nature that cures us, and that we must take care not to impede its action. Yes, that doctor was quite simply a sage, and it was the sage rather than the doctor to whom I appealed. I sent him the voluminous dossier on the question put together by the Ministry of the Interior. Did he even study that dossier? One might well doubt it, judging by the speed and above all by the tenor of his reply.

'Here is that reply. A three-page letter, handwritten, with a steel-nibbed pen in violet ink. In this letter, my old country doctor tells me . . . Oh, it will probably be best if I read it to you. Here it is, then:

'*Monsieur le Président de la République,*
My dear little François,

'I am proud and happy that you remember the modest practitioner who brought you into the world and kept an eye on you during your first years. To tell you the truth, I deserve very little credit, for you arrived and you grew of your own accord. And now you are turning to me – I who have not practised for so long – with a question of national importance and which, you tell me, has baffled the leading lights of the Faculty of Medicine. But it may be that these savants, by the very fact that they preside over the medical fraternity, are particularly badly-placed to be able to remedy the increasingly rapid escalation of medical costs? Seriously, Monsieur le Président, if you were looking for a way to spend less on armaments, would you go and ask the advice of our Chiefs of Staff? If I venture to reply to you, it is no doubt because it is a long time since I was a doctor, after having been very little of one during the whole of my career.

'The question you put to me, Monsieur le Président, reminds me of a cat I once had – a female cat, actually. Well, this cat was about to have kittens, and she took it into her head to have them in a thicket which extends as far as the eye can see on the other side of my garden wall. When I found her one day with a flat stomach and her eyes sparkling with innuendo, I soon realized what she was getting up to during her excursions to the neighbouring piece of ground, which I saw her embarking on every day. But I was careful not to interfere. Weeks and months went by. One morning I looked out of the window and saw my cat playing on one of the garden paths, surrounded by four mischievous kittens. This was probably the first time they had jumped over the wall after a childhood spent in the next-door thicket. I opened the door without taking any care, and went up to the little family. The mother-cat made a fuss of me, but the kittens scattered in all directions in a panic. Obviously. Why hadn't I thought of it? These little kittens, born and brought up away from men, were wild animals. Unless you tamed them patiently, they couldn't stand the presence of men.

'Tame them! I did everything I possibly could to that end. I tempted them with plates of cat food which I put down in the garden, nearer and nearer to the house. In this way I managed to entice one into my kitchen one day. And then I shut the door. The result was catastrophic. It began to howl as if it was being flayed alive. At the same time it leapt up on to the furniture, knocking over crockery and vases. Finally it hurled itself at the window, like a bird, and fell down half stunned. I took advantage of this to grab it and give it back its liberty.

'I am a little embarrassed, Monsieur le Président, at telling you such apparently trivial anecdotes. But unimportant incidents of the sort are close to life. They are life itself. What happens hour by hour in a garden is just as instructive as what one observes in a test-tube or retort in a laboratory, and when you appealed to me, it was no doubt in order to discover the point of view of a man of the soil, after having sought answers from the research that is carried on in vitro.

'The following weeks confirmed the impression left on me by that disastrous experiment: born in nature, those little kittens were beyond recovery. They had become permanently wild. I had occasion to speak of this with a neighbour who is a stock-breeder. He revealed this surprising fact: a calf or foal born in the fields will all its life be of a more difficult nature than one that has seen the light of day – if we can call it that – in the semi-darkness of a cattle shed. All breeders know this, and take good care not to let their females give birth in the open air.

'As you see, we are gradually approaching our subject. For what is true of the character of animals is even more so of the soul of human beings. Yes, the first impressions – sounds, lights, smells – that impinge on a child emerging from its mother's womb mark it for ever. It is like an irremediable curvature that will twist its character. Without being in any way a historian, I have made a few enquiries about the exact environment of the births of several men who made a *name for themselves. We know that Napoleon was born to the sound of the organ and amid the fumes of incense burnt at High Mass in celebration of the Assumption at the cathedral in Ajaccio. It is less well known that there was an earth tremor in Gori when Stalin was born. A terrible frost destroyed all the blossom on the fruit trees in the Braunau region on the night of 19 April 1889, which saw the birth of Adolf Hitler. The Ancients believed that the birth of a future great man was marked by wondrous events. We should no doubt invert the causal order and say that a wondrous event that occurs at the time of a child's birth may make him into an exceptional man.*

'Well, what is the considerable and almost universal revolution that has characterized obstetrics for the last fifty years? In the old days children were born in their parents' house. You yourself, Monsieur le Président – I remember your mother's bedroom, in which you uttered your first cry. And similarly, although no one really realized it, babies were born to peasants, workmen, artisans, fishermen or millionaires who preserved these labels as if they were tattooed in their innermost depths. Was this a good thing or a bad thing? I shall not try to decide. I mistrust the rather too frequent tendency of people of my age to prefer the things of the past. But in the last fifty years things have greatly changed. The practice of delivering babies in specialized clinics very quickly became the rule. True, hygiene and safety have enormously benefited from this new development. The number of accidents at birth has decreased in extremely heartening proportions. On the other hand, however, no one has measured the effect of this new environment on what I shall call the birth imprint. *Well yes, the birth imprint! This is a new concept that our learned obstetricians are going to have to make their computers swallow! For my part, I solemnly declare that a baby who comes into the world on an operating table and who breathes in the smell of disinfectants, hears the throbbing of electrical instruments and sees*

nothing around him but ghosts in white coats and antiseptic masks against a background of glossy walls in operating theatres – I declare that this baby, by virtue of this birth imprint, will always be inclined to . . . what is it called again? . . . clinicomania, medicomania, pharmacomania.

'Monsieur le Président, this is my suggested answer to your question: the exponential costs of our Social Security can only be explained by this clinical imprint imposed on newborn babies in the seconds, minutes and hours that follow their birth.

'So what can we do? Birth, love and death, it must be said, are not illnesses. They are the three great pivotal points of human destiny. The doctors must not be allowed to appropriate them. So let us begin by liberating births from the pharmaceutical miasmas that are poisoning them. This is what I suggest. When a woman is on the point of becoming a mother, she herself shall choose – as freely as she chooses her child's first name – the natural environment in which she would like to give birth and, by the same token, the birth imprint her child will receive. Everything will be organized so that she will be offered practically unlimited choice. In the coming years babies must be able to be born in all safety at the top of Mont Blanc or among the rocks of the Ile de Sein off Finistère, on a Pacific atoll or in the golden dunes of the Sahara, in the Hall of Mirrors in the Palace of Versailles, or on the third floor of the Eiffel Tower. And then we would see the new generations manifesting an inexhaustible variety of aspirations and vocations, instead of joining the sad queues at the doctor's or the chemist's.

'Yours very faithfully, Monsieur le Président, etc.'

The President put the pages of the letter down on a little table and looked, smiling, in the direction of the viewers.

'This then, my dear compatriots, is the strange and charming revolution I am suggesting to you. As from next spring, all measures will have been taken to enable the birth imprint to be as varied and even fanciful as future mothers could wish. But this very day, this evening, at this precise moment when I am speaking to you, we are going to inaugurate this new way of being born. So I am addressing my remarks to all the future mothers who are listening to me. Here is my telephone number: 42 92 81 00. If you are expecting a baby within the next few days, phone me at once. It is a direct line. The first future mother who calls me and expresses her wish, whatever it may be, that wish will be granted. I am waiting.'

Still smiling, the President rested his chin on his folded hands, and observed a silence. Almost at once the receiver by his side began to tinkle. Fifteen million viewers were then able to follow this strange dialogue, live.

'Hallo?' said a piping voice.

'Yes, this is the President of the Republic.'

'Good evening, Monsieur le Président.'

'Good evening, Madame.'

'Mademoiselle,' the piping voice corrected him.

'Mademoiselle. Mademoiselle . . . what name, if you please?'

'Marie.'

'Good evening, Mademoiselle Marie. So you are expecting to give birth. Do you know which day it's due?'

'They spoke of the twenty-fifth of December, Monsieur le Président.'

'Perfect, perfect. And what is the natural environment you are dreaming of for this birth?'

'A stable, Monsieur le Président. A stable with lots of straw. And also an ox and an ass.'

Despite his well-known self-control, the President could not prevent his eyes from opening wide in astonishment.

'A stable, some straw, an ox and an ass . . .' he repeated mechanically. 'Good, good, you shall have all that. Will you allow me one more question?'

'Of course, Monsieur le Président.'

'Have you had the sex of your child determined?'

'Yes, Monsieur le Président. It will be a girl.'

'Ah, bravo, a girl!' exclaimed the President with obvious relief. 'So much sweeter than a boy! So much calmer, so much more reassuring! Well, I should like to be her godfather, if you will accept me, and we shall call her Noëlle. Good evening to you all.'

Faust I,
King and Magus

'How is he, then?'

Faust I, King of Pergamum, stood erect, both terrible and trembling, as the Royal Physician came out of the Crown Prince's bedroom.

'Well! are you going to speak?' he burst out, as the doctor observed a dismayed silence.

'Alas!' he finally groaned.

'You don't mean to say . . .' the King stammered . . . 'you don't mean to say that the Dauphin . . .'

'Alas, yes!' sighed the Royal Physician.

The King pushed past the group of surgeons, apothecaries, herbalists and thaumaturges who were blocking the bedroom door, and rushed in. In the middle of a sordid disarray of syringes, phials, enemas, scalpels and bloodstained linen, the Dauphin was lying, his hands folded over his breast, white and cold as snow.

'Dead,' the King murmured. 'He is dead. Once again, the whole court of astrologers, alchemists, palmists, necromancers and suchlike phrenologists that I keep in my entourage have proved their ignorance. And I, after so many years of research and study, all that I know, is that I know nothing!'

In fact, from his earliest childhood the Prince of Pergamum had astonished his parents and teachers by his thirst for knowledge. For him, no book of spells was too hermetic, no foreign tongue too barbarous, no computations too intricate, no reasoning too subtle. It seemed as if any kind of difficulty in itself excited the insatiable curiosity of his mind, and his parents were perpetually afraid that this intellectual bulimia might lead to brain fever. When barely adolescent, it was he, and no one else, who for his personal use had perfected the art of parchment-making, for which Pergamum became renowned. This passion had not gone unobserved, and every day strange adventurers appeared at the palace, some bearing alleged secrets, others claiming to be experts in the magic arts or versed in the occult sciences, unwashed vehement prophets, covered in amulets, promising the infinite in exchange for a handful of gold. Faust I received them all, and often kept them at his court.

The Dauphin's bedroom opened on to a vast terrace overlooking the town. The King went out on to it and raised his eyes to the starlit sky. How many times, after heady discussions on entelechies and animal spirits, had he not thus cleansed his face and heart in the great, blue silence of the night!

His gaze suddenly came to rest on a luminous speck flickering somewhere between Betelgeuse and the Great Bear. This fantastic light seemed strangely alive in the midst of the vast, motionless amphitheatre of the firmament. It seemed as if, while slowly moving away towards the south, it was sending out messages, making signals to him, to *him*, the King of Pergamum, whose heart was bleeding. Then he remembered an old legend he had heard in his childhood.

'It's my son!' he exclaimed in awe, 'it's my beloved son who is taking flight with all speed. And he is sending me his last farewell, his last kisses, my dear son wants to tell me something, he is imploring me to understand. But what, oh God! Does he perhaps want me to follow him? Perhaps I should accompany him on his long migration towards the south? Why not? Is not travel the best of all remedies for life's sorrows?'

Two hours later a little caravan had been formed and the King of Pergamum, accompanied by a handful of faithful followers, started out on the strangest of all his voyages of discovery, towards he knew not what destination. He was content to follow the comet, which was slowly moving southwards.

The journey lasted for days and weeks. The little group reached the coast and embarked on a trireme. They put into port at Cyprus and then, as the comet's trajectory curved inwards towards the southeast, they directed their course to Caesarea. This was the first time that Faust I had set foot in Palestine. Quite naturally he made his way towards Jerusalem, then reigned over by Herod the Great, whose reputation for ferocity made the Mediterranean East tremble.

Herod received his royal visitor warmly and with great ceremony, as if to give the lie to his sinister reputation, of which he was well aware. And yet his fundamentally evil nature was almost naïvely displayed when he replied to the doubts and anguish which the King of Pergamum made known to him. The truth? He, Herod the Great, knew only one truth, and it had never failed him: a well-calculated mixture of violence and cunning. As for the savants, alchemists, astrologers and suchlike medicasters, he had a plethora of them in his palace and he used them whenever it suited his purpose. And he took his guest into the palace's secret rooms in which he had hidden a whole diabolical arsenal. He showed him phials whose contents were capable of annihilating an entire army, unguents that paralysed, drugs that made women sterile for ever. A certain liquid contained in an ordinary flask was capable of poisoning the water of a whole town. A gas enclosed in a phial could spread an appalling epidemic. Finally, with gestures full of loving respect, he showed him a glass eagle with outstretched wings: hurled down on to the houses from the top of a tower, it would explode as it broke, and cause as much destruction as an earthquake . . .

King Faust I, alone once again on the road with his little band of followers, was utterly perplexed. Was that what science was, then? Was the truth towards which reason, experimentation and research aspired nothing but that hell of suffering and death? Herod was all the more to be feared in that he knew so much more . . .

He raised his eyes to the sky, to question the stars once again. The dancing, laughing comet continued on its course southwards, and it seemed to be inviting him to keep following it. He set off again with his companions.

The mysterious road wound through mountains and valleys. 'Where are we going?' his Grand Chamberlain asked the King. For sole response, he gestured with his chin towards the strange comet scintillating ahead of them. However, it seemed to be slowing, stopping, even descending over the black mass of a village. Its dishevelled tail hung down over the earth like a hand of flame with a hundred fingers.

'What village is that?' asked the King.

'Bethlehem,' his guide replied. 'According to legend, King David was born there, a thousand years ago.'

They continued on their way. The comet was suspended like a chandelier above the houses, and its longest ray fell like a sheet of silver on to the roof of a sheepfold. Shepherds and villagers were crowding round the door. What a surprising sight there was inside! In a wooden manger lined with straw and made into a crib, a newborn baby was wriggling in his swaddling clothes. A greying man and a very young woman were watching over him, and around them there were quite naturally an ox, an ass, some goats and some sheep. There was no horse, because the horse is a rich man's beast.

All this might have been commonplace had there not also been, descending from the darkness of the blackened beams, a column of moving light, a radiant angel who, so it seemed, was presiding over the events of this intimate yet grandiose night, the complete opposite of Herod the Great's reception. It was Gabriel, the great master of these joyous ceremonies.

Faust I, King of Pergamum, knelt in front of the crib. He laid down his offering: one of the parchment scrolls that were the pride of the artisans of Pergamum.

'A book without content,' he explained, 'blank sheets – that is the derisory symbol of my life. It has been totally dedicated to the search for truth. And when I had come to the end of this quest, before my child's body, I had to acknowledge that I knew only one thing: I know that I know nothing. So I followed the fantastic star in which I wanted to see my son's soul. And I ask you, Lord: where is the truth?'

Naturally, the child did not answer this immense question with words. A newborn child does not make speeches. But he gave King Faust a different kind of answer, so much more convincing. His tender face turned towards him, his blue eyes opened very wide, a slight smile lit up his mouth. And there was so much naïve trust in that childish face, his gaze reflected an innocence so pure, that Faust suddenly felt all the shadows of doubt and anguish fading from his heart. Into the child's clear gaze, he felt himself toppling, as though into an abyss of light.

Angus

Because it is fragile and belated, spring in the Highlands of Scotland has an exquisitely delicate charm for the men and women of that land. With childlike impatience they await the return of the lapwings to the wild sky, the amorous call of the marsh grouse, and the first mauve patches of the crocuses on the rare grass on the hills. Every presage of spring after the long night of winter is welcomed like glad tidings, expected yet still surprising in its powerful verdancy. And the sudden explosion of the buds, the starry pink of the hawthorn bushes, the sea breeze softened by clouds of pollen touch the hearts of young and old alike, until they are close to tears.

Nowhere is the contrast between the roar of the equinoxial gales and the laments of the snowy owls in the first May nights more moving than on the lands of the Earl of Strathael. The black mass of the granite fortress in which the old Lord of Angus keeps vigil overlooks the verdant coombs with their bubbling, living springs, and an aspen wood with young foliage so delicate, so light that it seems to have been planted by some gardener's hand in order to offer the betrothed couple a translucent curtain for their rides.

It was through these gently undulating meadows that Colombella, the young daughter of the Lord of Angus, was riding that morning with her fiancé, Ottmar, Earl of Orkney. The two palfreys, then, were walking along shoulder to shoulder, their white breasts brushing aside the tall grass flecked with poppies, daisies and buttercups, and the young people were tenderly conversing. Ottmar had been studying in southern France, where the Count of Toulouse had made him welcome as a page at his court. He had taken part in the Floral Games, and learnt by heart the *Leys d'amors* compiled by the Consistory Court of the seven preservers of the poetry of the troubadours, 'le gai savoir'. Colombella, who had never left the Highlands, was listening, with somewhat timorous delight, to him singing the praises of a new art of living, born in those sun-blessed provinces, *la fin' amor*, or the art of loving and serving the lady of one's heart in courtly fashion.

The first essential, he was explaining, was to cleanse one's loving relationship of all material blemish. Almost all marriages are arranged by parents, aided by clerics, in accordance with their two fortunes, which must be brought together and united. No feeling can survive such a compromise. True, the ideal would be for both the betrothed to be equally poor, absolutely poor, but how could this ideal be approached outside the monastic life, which always strictly separates men from women?

Two wagtails, whirling and chirping, plummeted down between the horses' feet, then immediately took wing again and rejoined each other a little farther on.

'Look at the birds of the field,' the girl said. 'Could anyone be more unprovided for? And yet they form couples that last the whole year, and often far longer.'

'True,' Ottmar replied, 'but they merely unite for their procreative needs. The presence of the male and the female is necessary for the nest, the eggs, for their incubation and for feeding the brood. Whereas true love soars infinitely high above the exigences of procreation. Pure love can only be disincarnate, spiritualized, as sterile as the immaculate snow that covers the peak of Ben Nevis in winter.'

'Does that mean that bodies take no part in your *fin' amor*?' Colombella asked anxiously. 'Must one be a pure spirit to soar, as you advise, above the ordinary human condition?'

'Certainly not, but the body is only lovable thanks to the soul which transpierces it as a flame a lantern. If the flame is extinguished, the lantern is no more than a grey, dismal little cage.'

'But that light of the soul – how does it pass through the flesh and its enveloping garments?'

'There are the hands, there is the face, and above all there are the eyes, which are the windows of the soul, open to the lover, illuminating and warming him. Have you ever felt the cold darkness that disfigures the faces of the blind?'

Colombella's eyes, as bright and clear as running water, smiled at Ottmar's remarks.

'But,' the young man went on, 'above all, there are words. Love has a language of its own: poetry. A poet is a man who knows how to speak of love.'

They had now left the colourful meadows and entered the semi-obscurity of a wood. Ancient oaks mingled with giant beeches to form a cool, motionless vault. The young people had stopped and fallen silent, impressed by the great sylvan calm. The horses tossed their heads vehemently. A blue rock thrush flew up, uttering its trill of alarm. Something was happening. Indeed, a moment later they heard a light, hasty gallop on the stony path. Then a doe started from cover, stopped short in front of the riders, swerved violently to the left and disappeared among the bushes. Silence fell again, but the betrothed, who were familiar with the hunt and the woods, knew that a thrush whistling the alarm and a doe blindly started are signs of a huntsman's approach.

There were sounds of broken branches, of an enormous laugh, and finally the tall silhouette of a dark rider came into view. It was Tiphane, the powerful neighbouring lord. He was followed by his dwarf, Lucan, hunched up on a donkey. Tiphane was hunting on the lands of the Earl of Strathael, then. Courtesy demanded that he apologize for this. But Tiphane was not one to trouble himself with courtesy. He owned three castles, and his lands extended all the way to Cape Wrath. He lived alone with his dwarf in the gloomiest of his towers, his last wife having died of loneliness one winter during one of his interminable expeditions. His vassals fled at his approach. His neighbours avoided him. His immense fortune smelt only too strongly of violence and blood.

'I have lost a doe,' he said, 'but found a woman. Winsome and fresh, by my faith. I have lost nothing by the exchange!'

He laughed again. A frightening laugh. Ottmar intervened:

'Lord Tiphane, you have before you the Lady Colombella, daughter of the Lord of Angus, your neighbour,' he said, to dispel all misunderstanding.

But there was no misunderstanding. It seemed that Tiphane cared not a rap for the Lord of Angus. He ignored Ottmar, and addressed Colombella in insulting terms:

'Pretty doe, does not the sweetness of the spring inspire gallant thoughts in you? Will an old antlered stag, arriving unexpectedly in this part of the wood, find favour in your velvety eyes? True, he is no longer in the first flush of youth, but you may trust his strength and experience.'

He burst out laughing as he approached the couple.

'Lord Tiphane,' said Ottmar, 'you forget yourself. For the last time, I must ask you to respect this young lady.'

Tiphane seemed not to hear what Ottmar had said. He dismounted. He laid his hunting gloves on his saddle, and his baldric with its dagger. He even removed his heavy velvet doublet. Then he advanced, in his loose embroidered shirt, and gallantly held out a gnarled hand, weighed down with bracelets and rings, to Colombella. Ottmar could bear no more.

'Lord Tiphane,' he cried, 'I warn you that if you take one more step towards my fiancée I will cut off your ears!'

He drew his sword, but immediately fell to the ground. Lucan, who had climbed into the branches of a nearby tree, had just dropped down on to him. The two men went rolling over on the ground. But the dwarf leapt up. A rope attached to his left foot encircled Ottmar's neck, and the dwarf pulled on the other end with both hands. Tiphane contemplated the scene with a smile. Colombella, white as a corpse, became faint with horror. There was a lengthy silence, which lasted as long as the young man's death throes. Then Tiphane seized Colombella by the wrist. He was no longer smiling. He dragged her out of her saddle.

'Well, now, pretty doe,' he said, 'come and do your duty as a female. It's the rutting season.'

* * *

As the sun rose in the sky, so anguish descended into the heart of the old Lord of Angus. It was now four hours since his daughter and future son-in-law had gone out alone on their palfreys. They should have been back long before. Angus had absolute confidence in Ottmar. And no one had ever met either brigands, or marauders, or lost soldiers in the neighbouring countryside and woods. Why, then, should he tremble? But tremble he did. He felt that the glorious sky was concealing fearful shadows under its tent of azure and gold.

Suddenly, Angus shivered. He could hear the sound of a horse's footsteps on the cobbles of the castle courtyard. They were back! But why could he hear only one horse? Angus went to a window. He saw a groom run to meet a riderless horse. He recognized Colombella's piebald mare. Calamity had struck Strathael.

There were shouts, calls, orders. Angus placed himself at the head of a small band of men and they rode out in search of the missing pair. The couple had last been seen going off in the direction of the woods that, far to the east, joined the lands of Strathael to the immense estate belonging to Lord Tiphane. No one uttered that fearsome name, but it was present in the minds of Angus and his companions. They did not need to search long among the trees and bushes before they came upon the place of the double crime. Along a path studded with campanulas, under an oak tree, Ottmar was lying with a red furrow round his neck. A little farther off, naked, bloodstained, haggard, they found the girl, who allowed them to take her away without a word. Had she become mute or mad? Angus realized that it would be useless to try to question her. Her face was an immobile, withered mask that imposed silence. Bertram, the Master of the Strathael Hunt, examined the traces of the horses' hooves that crossed each other on the soft earth. One trail undoubtedly came from the east, the direction of Tiphane's castle. Even more evident were the little hoof prints of a donkey that led in the same direction. And no one was unaware that Tiphane was frequently accompanied by a dwarf riding astride a donkey.

The Lord of Angus knew all this, but no one dared ask him what were his intentions. He was alone, old, and ill. He could not dream of challenging Tiphane as he would have done thirty years earlier. As for bringing him to justice before his peers for his horrible crime, Colombella's evidence would be necessary for that. And she was in no state to provide it. Would she ever be? And if she did recover the necessary strength, would she accept the terrible humiliation of being confronted with her assailant? Violators almost always find their salvation in the modesty of their victims.

The next morning a man appeared at the castle leading a horse by the bridle. He was one of Tiphane's men. This horse had been found wandering in the vicinity of his domain. Did it come from Strathael? The Lord of Angus's men recognized Ottmar's horse. To Angus, this restitution was yet another insult. But what did it matter! His injury was so severe that his vengeance must be given time to mature. He did not yet know what this vengeance would be, but Tiphane could wait. The more time passed, the more cruel would be his punishment.

*　　　　*　　　　*

Colombella recovered her powers of speech, but she spoke only sparingly, and in a murmur. No one, however – not even her father – dared make any allusion in her presence to the double crime. Did she even remember it? Everything in her conduct seemed to indicate that her memory had effaced the image of that beautiful spring morning when she had been discussing *la fin' amor* with her betrothed.

Her memory, perhaps, but not her flesh, for at the end of the summer it became apparent that she was expecting a child. This was a second misfortune, even more terrible than the first, for it was a pledge to the future. This fruit swelling inside her was like an incurable malignant tumour, like a new rape repeated every hour. She no longer left her apartments. She barely ate. And the more emaciated she grew, the more monstrous her pregnancy became. People gave credence to the official story – which deceived no one at the castle – according to which Ottmar had secretly married her and then been killed by marauders. Shortly before Christmas she gave birth to a son.

'He is innocent,' she murmured to her father, who was bending over her. 'Forgive him for existing.'

The next day she died. The Lord of Angus had the child baptized on the day of his mother's funeral, wishing thereby to mark the curse that lay heavy upon him. He had him christened James, and sent him to a peasant wet-nurse, promising himself never to see him again.

As the years went by, he could not keep his promise. This child was his grandson, his sole heir. More and more frequently, when he went riding alone or with Bertram, he found himself going towards the farm where James was growing up. He had him pointed out amongst the swarm of grimy, sturdy children playing in the yard. He watched him with horror. He was Tiphane's son, the living proof of the double crime of that accursed spring. And yet he was innocent. 'Forgive him for existing!' Colombella had entreated on her deathbed.

One day – the child must have been about six – the Lord of Angus had him brought to him in order to get a closer look at him. Although he had the manners of a little peasant, there was some quality about him that distinguished him from the other bastards at the farm. Angus looked him in the eyes. Through the blond hair falling over his face, the child solemnly met his gaze. Angus could not repress a sob: they were Colombella's eyes – eyes as bright and clear as running water – that were gazing at him. That day he took the child back to the castle.

He entrusted his education as a future knight to Bertram. They sent for a Shetland pony for him to ride. His short legs were spread-eagled round the barrel-shaped belly of the tiny horse, but he shouted for joy as he urged it to a gallop. He also learned to groom, feed and harness his mount.

It was when observing the spirit with which he wielded the backsword against a much older boy, and the courage with which he took the blows he was struck, that the Lord of Angus for the first time conceived of the form his vengeance against Tiphane – which was never out of his thoughts – might take. It would be James himself who would punish his rapist father, thus avenging his mother. The old lord found continuing satisfaction in the simplicity and severity of this solution. To make a child whom he both loved and hated confront the monster would be to put the matter in God's hands, to rely on God's judgment to cut the knot that was strangling him. No doubt the combat would be terribly unequal, even if they waited until James was old enough to be dubbed a knight. But it was precisely this inequality that would oblige divine justice to manifest itself, if only through a miracle. And Angus's pride was inflamed at the idea of this dilemma in which he was going to place God: to allow Tiphane to commit a third crime, but this time against his own son, or to reverse the natural order and cause the child to triumph against the giant.

His age and the state of his health gave him no hope of being able to witness the ordeal himself. But he thought he might at least live long enough until James was of an age to be told the terrible secret of his birth and the exploit that honour demanded of him. But this was not to be. James was not yet seven years old when the Lord of Angus felt his forces mortally declining. When he had put all his affairs in order, he demanded to be left alone with his sole heir. And then, without burdening him with explanations, he made him swear on a crucifix that he would challenge and kill their neighbour Lord Tiphane in single combat as soon as he had been dubbed a knight. This thought must never leave his heart, but he must never, before the appointed hour, allow his mouth to betray it by a single word. Educated in an atmosphere of mystery and heroism, the child swore this oath without showing any surprise.

The Lord of Angus died and, according to his wishes, Bertram assumed James's guardianship and the running of the estate. Bertram, then, continued to be a father and friend to the child. And yet James never divulged anything, and kept the oppressive secret to himself. Sometimes, in the middle of a game or dance he was enjoying with youths and girls of his own rank, he would grow serious, fall silent and seem to be far away. If he was asked, 'What is the matter, my Lord? What sad thought is suddenly engrossing you?' he would shake his head, laugh, and rejoin the merry throng. But his friends were worried, because they knew that he was naturally of a happy-go-lucky disposition and that only a dark presentiment could thus cast a shadow over his good humour.

In the meantime he devoted all his energies to making progress in the profession of arms, and it was clear that he was particularly desirous of preparing himself for single combat, for fighting man to man. He showed such ferocity in these encounters that his companions, who at first saw it simply as a game, soon bowed out, fearing that they would receive, or be forced to inflict, some serious injury. Bertram's remonstrations were to no avail. When he raised the vizor of his helmet, James would reveal a distraught face and he seemed resolved to moderate his fervour, but the moment the vizor fell again it was as if there was a different man behind it, one of homicidal brutality. And Bertram could not repress a dark premonition.

Came the day most eagerly awaited by every young squire, that of his investiture as a knight. According to custom, James was not to be the only one to receive his knight's sword. Two other adolescents were to be armed with him, and they were David, Marquess of Stirling, and Malcolm, Duke of Argyll. The ceremony and the celebrations that followed would be all the more glorious in that they would be shared by three friendly neighbouring houses.

On the eve of this solemn day the three young men had made their confession after sundown and then spent the night in prayer and meditation in the castle chapel. The three swords and the six golden spurs had been placed on the altar. In the morning they had taken communion in both kinds, and then gone to rest for a while. At midday they gave a ceremonial welcome to the Earl of Aberdeen and the Bishop of the Cathedral of Saint Machar, who had come especially to preside over the knighting. The arms and uniforms were gleaming in the bright sun, as was the apparel of the crowd of relations and friends gathered in the main courtyard of the castle. The bishop blessed the swords and spurs. Then each of the young squires came up in turn to stand in front of the Earl of Aberdeen, who with the help of two attendants girded on their baldrics, fastened their spurs, and then gave them the *colée* on the back of the neck. After that he said a short prayer, in which he asked God, who authorized the use of the glaive to curb the wickedness of evil men, to help the new knights never to use it unjustly. Finally he turned to David and urged him never to fight in a vindictive spirit. He particularly enjoined Argyll to act always without selfish motives but with generosity. And he reminded James that a knight must feel absolutely bound by his oath, and always honour his word.

Chance being an invention of the miscreant, this exhortation could only be attributed to Providence, for it was unthinkable that Aberdeen could have had any knowledge of James's origins or of his secret. This secret was to be revealed in the following week, and Bertram was the first to know of it. James sent for him and read aloud to him – in a voice that was firm and imperious, even though the silvery notes of adolescence could still be heard in it – a short communication he had just written:

> *Lord Tiphane, now that I have been created a knight, I am finally empowered to keep an oath I swore as a child to my grandfather, the Lord of Angus, as he lay dying. I swore to kill you. I challenge you, therefore, to single combat, in a place and according to the procedure that you will agree with the bearer of this message. The sooner the better.*
>
> *Signed: James of Angus, Earl of Strathael.*

*

Bertram was aghast. So that was it! That was James's terrible secret, which had hung over his entire childhood like a vulture, and which had now swooped down on him! For he had no chance, not the slightest chance, of defeating Tiphane in single combat. Tiphane was a giant. His strength, skill and ferocity made the whole West tremble. The sixteen-year-old James, with his blond curls, his girlish arms and his voice that had barely broken was going to meet certain death. His youthful foolhardiness was challenging the mountain, the storm, the volcano. Bertram could not restrain his tears.

'Why are you weeping?' James asked.

'It would need a miracle,' Bertram replied.

'There will be a miracle!' James asserted.

For such is the faith of a Christian knight that he lives on an equal footing with God, the Virgin Mary, Jesus, and all the saints.

*   *   *

Tiphane was pacing round and round in his granite tower like a wild beast in its cage. With the passing years, everything that had given a pungent, piquant taste to his life had come to seem grey and insipid. Whether it was cutting the throat of a stag at bay, violating a girl he had come upon unawares in the fields, hanging a serf found guilty of poaching, despoiling a rich traveller, ransacking the house of a litigious neighbour, burning a scholar suspected of witchcraft, nothing really amused him any more. Even his expeditions to far-off lands seemed tedious. Neither the raging sea, nor the burning sands of the desert, nor the icy wastes of the far North could restrain the disgust by which he was submerged. He who had so long since buried his last wife, and whose days and nights had been filled by the laughter and vociferations of his fellow gallowsbirds – he was now suddenly discovering solitude. No one. He had no one with him any more. No one was left but Lucan, his hunchbacked dwarf, his evil genius, the accomplice of all his crimes and the witness of all his triumphs.

Lucan was now standing in front of him, a heavily-sealed manuscript in his hand.

'Now what is it?' Tiphane growled.

'Your neighbour has written to you, Lord Tiphane.'

'What does he want of me?'

'To kill you. In single combat.'

'At last!' cried Tiphane. 'Someone who wishes me well! I was dying of inaction. I was wondering whether I should have to go to China or Arabia to find a fight. And here is someone offering me a first-class diversion on my very doorstep. How extremely obliging of him. And what is the name of this neighbour who is so eager to divert me?'

'Angus, Earl of Strathael.'

'James!'

'James,' Lucan confirmed, scrutinizing his master's face, furrowed with wrinkles and sabre cuts, that he knew so well.

'James,' repeated Tiphane, astounded. 'So this is the vengeance of that old devil Angus. I have been wondering for years what he was going to manage to invent. I can hear him now, guffawing in his grave.'

Lucan waited, holding his breath. Because for the last ten years, on Tiphane's orders, he had had spies watching James's every move. He was his son, his only child, his sole heir.

'And he wants to kill me,' Tiphane growled. 'But after all, that's in the order of things. Good blood cannot lie. I too would have been happy to kill my father. The thing is, though, one does not kill a Tiphane just like that. We are anything but bleating sheep. And personally, I have not the slightest wish to die.'

'He is sixteen. Anyone would take him for fourteen,' said Lucan. 'You will make short work of him!'

'Short work? But what makes you think I want him to die?' yelled Tiphane. 'No, no, no. He demands a fight. He shall have it. But he will learn that one does not raise a hand against a Tiphane with impunity. I shall teach him a pretty sharp lesson. In front of the whole county, I shall wrest off his basinet and pull his ears. A spanking, a good spanking, that's what he'll get, the impertinent young bastard. What's more, the better to mock him, I shall go to the combat bareheaded.'

'Bareheaded?'

'Yes, bareheaded. In that way he will see my lion's mane and my prophet's beard. Fledgling that he is, he will be rooted to the spot by my eagle's gaze under my shaggy eyebrows. Ha ha ha!'

And the castle servants, hearing their lord's enormous laugh, trembled as they wondered what new diabolical scheme he was concocting with his dwarf.

*   *   *

Twelve horn blowers wearing red dalmatics had announced in the hamlets, the villages and the burghs that the two lords were to meet on Sunday at the eleventh hour in the lists set up in the heathland along the coast. So there was an extraordinary multitude of people and, as the day promised to be fine, families had planned to have lunch and then dance in the open air.

James's levity dismayed Bertram. It seemed as if the imminence of the resolution of the drama of his life – whatever it might turn out to be – relieved him of all care. He had invited whole droves of boys and girls of his own age, and the days preceding the combat had been nothing but a succession of games and diversions. Was that the way he intended to prepare himself for the terrible ordeal he was about to undergo? Having managed with great difficulty to take him aside, Bertram had put this question to him with some vehemence. Suddenly becoming serious, James had replied: 'I have entrusted my fate into the hands of God. Could he abandon a knight who is simply honouring his word?' With his total faith, he thus unwittingly became one with his grandfather's vision. Bertram had lowered his head. And yet he could not contain his indignation when on the Sunday, after he had heard Mass and taken communion, James turned away the squires who wanted to help him gird on his armour and don his helmet.

'No,' he said. 'I have heard that Lord Tiphane is proposing to fight bareheaded in order to humiliate me. I shall do even better.

Not only shall I go bareheaded, but barelegged too, in the manner of the ancestors of my clan.'

No one could make him go back on his decision. Bertram, too, finally resigned himself to it. He felt himself to be the impotent witness of the unravelling of a mystery whose majestic enactment was beyond all common sense and reason. Besides, James, haloed with light, no longer obeyed, no longer heard anything, as if borne along by the irresistible force of his destiny.

This was indeed how the crowd saw him when he entered the lists, greeted by the golden fanfare of the trumpets. On his little dapple-grey horse that was prancing in a ray of sunshine, the blond, blue and pink child, clad in silk and tartan, had the unreal radiance of an apparition. Was it because he was doomed to die, or because he was surrounded by angels? Both, perhaps.

At the other end of the combat area the muffled roar of drums announced Tiphane's entry. He was of truly monstrous stature, clad in iron, riding a warhorse that was as black as night. But he had kept his word, and above the throatpiece of his armour his head appeared, with its grey bush of hair and beard and two deep-set, glaring, tawny eyes. The contrast between the two adversaries was startling – so startling that a murmur of protest rose from the crowd. Had anyone ever seen so unfairly unequal a combat? Voices could even be heard crying: 'Enough! Stop! It's a crime!' Then silence fell, for the Duke of Elgin, who was presiding over the joust, had just waved his short white baton, the signal for the fight to begin.

*   *   *

Tiphane continued to advance, walking his horse, his lance raised. James had lowered his, and charged him at a full gallop. There was a first clash, but it was attenuated because the point of James's lance had glanced off Tiphane's right shoulder-piece. From this first engagement, it was clear that James was not aiming at his adversary's unprotected head, an act of reckless chivalry that robbed him of his sole chance of winning. The two riders turned their horses, but this time Tiphane put his charger at a canter and lowered his lance. He even lowered it so far that it seemed that he was suddenly aiming at James's horse. The crowd murmured. According to the rules of knightly combat, it is a felony to wound an adversary's horse deliberately. The black horse gathered speed. James came up at full tilt. There was a kind of thud. The dapple-grey horse staggered, but the crowd immediately saw its saddle flying up into the air, and James rolling over in the dust. Everyone realized that Tiphane had struck the pommel of the saddle with such force that the girth had given way. According to etiquette, Tiphane should have dismounted and the fight should have continued with swords. He did no such thing. He waited, motionless, while the squires mastered James's horse and put a new saddle on it. As for James, no one was allowed to go to his aid until the judge had declared the joust to be over. He had nimbly picked himself up and dashed to his mount. Meanwhile, everyone could see that blood was flowing from his left arm on to his hand, a wound no doubt more awkward than serious. Tiphane prepared himself to bear the brunt of a new assault, and indeed James rushed at him, lance foremost. But his weapon glanced off Tiphane's lance, and James, carried forward by his own momentum, soon found himself stopped by the barrier at the end of the lists. He immediately turned his horse.

*　　　*　　　*

How much longer would this unequal contest last? Once again James repeated his assault on the giant, but already his little horse, all reflexes and jerks, was no longer displaying the same energy. Was Tiphane counting on the exhaustion of the rider and his mount? James's lance struck Tiphane's breastplate so impetuously that it broke into several pieces. Tiphane had not moved. James rode over towards his attendants, who came running up with another lance. But as he was making his way back to the barrier, he saw Tiphane bend over his horse's neck. There was a murmur of stupefaction among the spectators. In fact the giant was toppling forwards. His forehead was just about to touch his horse's mane when he slipped sideways and fell to the ground with a great clanking of metal. His attendants rushed to his aid, while James dismounted. He bent over the great body lying there like a recumbent statue on a tomb, and saw that one of the fragments of his lance – its point, perhaps – was deeply lodged in Tiphane's right orbit.

He remounted his horse and was greeted with a tremendous ovation. The enthusiasm showed the extent of the anxiety the people had felt for him. Hats went flying in the air. Children laden with flowers jumped into the lists and ran up to him. He was almost carried out in triumph, while six men laboured to put Tiphane on a stretcher. It seemed to James that a grey veil that had been concealing everything from him had just been torn to shreds. At last he was able to see the walls of the houses adorned with tapestries, the windows decorated with armorial bearings, the pennons flying on flagstaffs gay with bunting, and above all, that crowd, those men and women in their best clothes giving voice to their joy. His friends crowded round him, ardent, youthful courtiers. How well suited to youth are luck and victory! How handsome he was on his little dapple-grey horse, with his grazed knees and that arm covered in blood! In truth, he was radiant, like a figure in a stained-glass window. A peal of little bells came from the belfry of the nearby church. James stopped, raised his hand with a smile, and said:

'It's Sunday, it's midday, and I have defeated Tiphane!'

And everyone understood that at that moment the Sabbath, the noonday hour and his triumph came together in an unsurpassable pinnacle. Nothing could ever be so perfect again.

*   *   *

During the evening, and late into the night, Strathael Castle was ablaze with all the lights of an unequalled celebration. The tables were weighed down with venison, fruit and delicacies. The cup-bearers were lavish with French and Italian wines. Minstrels, jugglers and acrobats had been summoned. There was even an animal exhibitor who had great success when he produced a bear and a monkey together. James presided over these rejoicings as if in a dream. Either he did not feel his fatigue, or it served to complete his intoxication with the music, the liquors, the blazing hearths and the smiles that flourished under his gaze.

Midnight was approaching when a servant bent over him. A stranger was demanding to be heard forthwith. Where had he come from? From Lord Tiphane's castle. It seemed that he was the bearer of a message. A message from Tiphane! This was a sensational surprise! James stood up. Silence fell. The dancers were requested to return to their places.

'Tell him to come in!' James ordered.

There was an anxious moment. Without admitting it to themselves, everyone was expecting to see the giant appear in person, in his armour, his face covered in the blood from his blinded eye. But it was Lucan the dwarf who came in, and he was so ugly that it was even worse. He gave not a glance at the guests and went straight up to James.

'Earl of Strathael, Lord of Angus,' he said, 'I have some important and sad news to convey to you: Lord Tiphane has succumbed to his wound. It is nevertheless he who has sent me to you, for despite the cruel torments of his last hours, he dictated a message that I am to read to you.'

He unrolled the manuscript he had brought, and in his discordant voice began to read the communication which was at the same time a confession, a will, and a challenge.

'James of Strathael, I feel that life is leaving me because of the wound you inflicted on me. This is a good thing. I was afraid of dying of decrepitude and decay. That would have been the worst punishment in a life filled with cut and thrust. A well-deserved punishment, no doubt, if I am to believe the chaplain to whom I have just made my confession. The good man was quite upset at the account of my exploits, my deeds of valour or of malfeasance. Although, heaven knows, I only told him a quarter of the tenth part of them, otherwise we should still be at it, and then, one has one's sense of shame, does one not? To have done with all

this religious humbug, I must tell you that just before
absolving me of all these crimes, whether confessed or not, he
asked me to pronounce an act of contrition. That was the
very least he could ask. Only the thing is, of all possible acts,
the act of contrition is certainly the one I am the least capable
of performing. Repent – me? By heaven! I've led the life I
have led. There's no more to be said! God will either take me
the way I am, or cast me into outer darkness. I greatly
surprised my Capuchin friar when I confessed that of all the
blood I have caused to flow so copiously in the last half-
century, only the blood I saw on your arm when you picked
yourself up earlier has ever given me distress. I had to unseat
you though, didn't I, but how was I to do you no harm when,
with your harebrained conceit, you were wearing neither
breastplate, nor hauberk, nor thigh-pieces, nothing but wool
and silk? I did my best, but I still reproach myself for that
blood. Because, you know, while I have nothing against a
son killing his father – that's in the order of things, and I
swear to you that if I had ever had a chance to kill mine, I
should not have failed to do so – the little scrap of moral
principle that I possess does not allow a father to kill his son.
For you are my son, James, I might as well reveal that
without further delay. It is a very simple, very sad story
which does honour to no one. Your grandfather did not like
me. That devout man had heard too many tales about me.
And yet I used to humour him. For years he had absolutely
no cause for complaint about me as a neighbour. I had
something in mind. I asked him for the hand of his daughter
Colombella, as soon as she became fifteen. He refused
indignantly. The difference in age, he said; my previous
wives, whose disappearance had given rise to malicious
rumours; my escapades, which were sometimes a little
dubious, I must admit. We parted, never to meet again. He
had other plans for Colombella – a young nobleman from
the Orkneys who had just come back from the court at
Toulouse, his head filled with stuff and nonsense. I was

furious, but, as God is my witness, I was not plotting anything definite against my neighbours. Then one spring morning, the luck of the chase brought me face to face with the betrothed. I acted as my blood and acrimony dictated. Did I do wrong? No doubt. But what was done was done, and the result was a bastard—you, James, and my goodness, that's not so bad. I said bastard. That was true only a moment ago. It is no longer so, for I hereby legitimize you, and make you the sole heir of all my titles, properties and possessions. I die happy, knowing that my heritage and my name are in your young hands. We have only seen each other long enough to exchange a few blows, the last of which killed me. I wish you a little more happiness with your own progeny. Not only do I die happy, but also absolved, for I have not finished the story of my sole and last confession. My good Capuchin was sorely grieved at being unable to give me absolution in the absence of any act of contrition on my part. And so was I, at that, because I felt sorry for him, and anyway I wanted to make an end of it. He then told me that there did exist a form of absolution without an act of contrition, absolution in articulo mortis. *This is given to the dying when their consciousness is already half-dimmed. All I had to do, then, was to enter into my death agony, which I did forthwith, for just as long as it took him to mumble his paternosters. I have recovered my wits since then, because I needed to speak to you, but I now feel I have come to the end of my strength and I think my agony — the real one, this time — will soon begin. The nail you stuck in my eye — do you realize that it is still there? No surgeon has dared to extract this splinter which has penetrated to my brain. It is the finger of God, my confessor — him again — told me. It must be admitted that Providence sometimes acts in a rather facetious manner. But tell me, my boy, this spike you shot into the air in such a way that it would fall precisely into my orbit — admit that you had*

*heated it red-hot beforehand! Because, you see, it is
burning my entire head. It is spreading showers of
sparks all through my skull. It is not a nail, or a splinter,
or a spike, it is a flare, it is Greek fire, it is hell. James
Tiphane, I . . . you . . . I . . .'*

Lucan fell silent and looked at James as he carefully rolled up the
manuscript. Tiphane's son was as pale as a wax candle. The
golden mist of his intoxication had dissipated and given way to a
bitter, desolate lucidity. He had the sour taste of real things in his
mouth. He lowered his eyes to the ravaged table, strewn with the
remains of the feast, and it seemed to him that this confusion of
faded flowers, squashed cakes, overturned goblets and soiled
napkins symbolized in some sordid way the debris of his youth.
One by one, the words transmitted by the dwarf had robbed him
of his illusions. So his father had violated his mother. He himself
was no more than the bastard of this crime. His combat against
Tiphane had been a false combat, so his splendid victory was only
a false victory. And he had ingloriously killed his own father. But
he had also learned that he was legitimate, and that by direct line
of descendance he had become the most powerful overlord in the
Highlands of Scotland. Thousands of peasants, artisans, burgh-
ers and soldiers expected his aid, his protection and his orders.
His unclouded adolescence, full of songs and daydreams, had
suddenly come to an end. In the space of a few minutes, of a few
words, he had become a man.

NOTE

On 22 May 1985, the hundredth anniversary of the death of
Victor Hugo was celebrated with great ceremony. Having meekly
immersed himself in his works, I reread with greater admiration
than ever *L'Aigle du casque* (*The Eagle on the Helmet*), a poem of
about four hundred lines which forms part of his *La Légende des
siècles* (*The Legend of the Centuries*). It is the combat of David and
Goliath, but without the supernatural biblical element. This
time, in fact, the giant is not overwhelmed by his puny adversary.

The logic of the forces confronting each other operates mercilessly: the child is put to flight, and the giant follows him and cuts his throat.

Yet from the very first lines, I was alerted by a considerable 'blank' deliberately left by the author: why does the old Lord of Angus demand on his deathbed that his six-year-old grandson should swear to kill the neighbouring lord, Tiphane?

> *The background, no one knows. The obscure past conceals*
> *From memory of man the origin, the cause*
> *Of the fights at Nineveh, of the Aegina wars . . .*

Nevertheless. The reader wonders, questioning both himself and this 'obscure past'. All the more so as a second mystery follows, deepening the first. Little James is brought up by his grandfather Angus. He is an orphan. What became of his parents? But, the reader wonders, what if these two questions were really only one? What if these mysteries, instead of deepening each other, explained each other? We need only imagine that Tiphane must be killed by James because he bears an overwhelming responsibility for the death of his parents.

This is the supposition that we have made. But only to find straightaway that the story was taking a very different turn from that reported by Victor Hugo, the first victim of the change being the helmet eagle itself, which flew away not at the end of the story but no doubt before it even began. We entreat the shade of Victor Hugo to forgive us for our liberty, and to be kind enough to consider this tale as a humble act of homage to the greatest of all French poets.

M.T.

Pierrot or
The Secrets of the Night

Two little white houses stood opposite each other in the village of Pouldreuzic. One was the laundry. No one could remember the real name of the laundress, for everyone called her Columbine because of her snowy-white dress which made her look like a dove. The other house was Pierrot's bakery.

Pierrot and Columbine had grown up together on the benches of the village school. They were so often together that everyone imagined that later they would marry. And yet life had separated them, when Pierrot had become a baker and Columbine a laundress. Inevitably, a baker has to work at night, so that the whole village may have fresh bread and hot croissants in the morning. A laundress works during the day, so that she can hang out her linen in the sun. Even so, they might have met at twilight, in the evening when Columbine was getting ready to go to bed and Pierrot was getting up, or in the morning when Columbine's day was starting and Pierrot's night was ending.

But Columbine avoided Pierrot, and the poor baker was eating his heart out with sorrow. Why did Columbine avoid Pierrot? Because her former schoolmate reminded her of all sorts of unpleasant things. Columbine only liked the sun, the birds, and the flowers. She only blossomed in the summer, in the daylight. Whereas the baker, as we have said, lived mostly at night, and for Columbine night was only darkness peopled by terrifying beasts like wolves and bats. And then she preferred to close her door and her shutters, to snuggle up under her duvet and go to sleep. But that wasn't all, because Pierrot's life was spent between two other, even more alarming darknesses, that of his cellar and that of his oven. Who knew whether there weren't rats in his cellar? And isn't there an expression: 'as dark as an oven?'

It must be admitted, though, that Pierrot looked the part. Perhaps because he worked at night and slept during the day, he had a round, pale face which made him look like the full moon. His big, watchful, astonished eyes gave him the appearance of an owl, as did his loose, baggy clothes, white with flour. Pierrot was shy, taciturn, loyal and reticent. He preferred the winter to the summer, solitude to company, and rather than speak – which he found difficult, and wasn't very good at – he preferred to write, which he did by candlelight, with an enormous pen, addressing long letters to Columbine which he never sent, as he was sure she wouldn't read them.

What did Pierrot write in his letters? He tried to disabuse Columbine. He explained to her that the night wasn't what she thought.

Pierrot knew the night. He knew that it isn't a black hole, any more than his cellar and his oven were. At night, the river sings more loudly and more clearly, and it scintillates with thousands and thousands of silvery scales. The foliage that the tall trees shake against the dark sky is all sparkling with stars. The night breezes are more profoundly imbued with the smell of the sea, of the forest and of the mountain than are the day's effluvia, which are impregnated with the work of men.

Pierrot knew the moon. He knew how to look at it. He could see that it isn't just a white disc as flat as a plate. Because he looked at it so carefully and with such affection, he had been able to see with the naked eye that it has contours, that it is actually a ball – like an apple, like a pumpkin; – and moreover, that it is not smooth but nicely sculpted, modelled, undulating – like a landscape with its hills and its valleys, like a face with its wrinkles and its smiles.

Yes, Pierrot knew all that, because of his dough which, after he had kneaded it for a long time and secretly impregnated it with yeast, needed two hours to rest and rise. Then he went out of his bakehouse. Everyone was asleep. He was the clear conscience of the village. He walked through all its streets and alleyways, his big, round eyes wide open while the others were asleep, the men, women and children who, when they awoke, would eat the hot croissants he had made for them. He passed under Columbine's closed windows. He had become the village's night watchman, Columbine's protector. He imagined the young girl sighing and dreaming in the moist whiteness of her big bed, and when he raised his pale face to the moon, he wondered whether that soft, round shape floating above the trees in a shroud of fog was that of a cheek, a breast, or, better still, a buttock.

No doubt everything could have gone on like this for a long time if, one fine summer's morning, a funny sort of vehicle, completely covered in flowers and birds and pulled by a man, had not made its entrance into the village. It was something between a caravan and a fairground stall, because on the one hand it was quite clear that you could shelter and sleep in it, and on the other hand it glistened with bright colours, and gaudily-painted curtains floated all around it like flags. On top of the vehicle was a glossy sign:

HARLEQUIN
House Painter

The man – lithe, vivacious, with rosy cheeks and curly red hair – was dressed in a kind of leotard composed of little motley diamonds. There were all the colours of the rainbow in it, plus a few more, but none of the diamonds was either black or white. He stopped his cart in front of Pierrot's bakery and pursed his lips in disapproval as he examined its bare, dull façade which bore only these two words:

PIERROT BAKER

He rubbed his hands with a confident air, and began to knock on the door. It was broad daylight, as we have said, and Pierrot was fast asleep. Harlequin had to drum on the door for a long time before it opened to reveal a Pierrot who was paler than ever and tottering with fatigue. Poor Pierrot! He really did look like an owl, all white, dishevelled, bewildered, his eyes blinking in the merciless summer light. What was more, before Harlequin had even had time to open his mouth, a great burst of laughter rang out behind him. It was Columbine, who was watching the scene from her window, with a heavy iron in her hand. Harlequin turned round, saw her, burst out laughing in his turn, and Pierrot found himself alone and sad in his lunar clothing confronted by those two children of the sun, brought together by their common gaiety. Then he lost his temper and, his heart aching with jealousy, he slammed the door in Harlequin's face and went back to bed, but it is highly unlikely that he got back to sleep very quickly.

As for Harlequin, he crossed the street to the laundry, where Columbine had disappeared. He looked for her. She reappeared, but at another window, then disappeared again before Harlequin had time to get close. It looked as if she was playing hide-and-seek with him. Finally the door opened, and Columbine came out carrying a huge basket of clean linen. Followed by Harlequin, she went into her garden and began to hang her linen out to dry. It was white linen, exclusively. As white as Columbine's dress. As white as Pierrot's costume. But Columbine never exposed her white linen to the moon, only to the sun, the same sun that makes every colour shine, in particular those of Harlequin's costume.

Harlequin, the glib talker, held forth to Columbine. Columbine answered him. What did they say to each other? They talked about clothes. Columbine about white clothes. Harlequin about coloured clothes. For the laundress, white went without saying. Harlequin did his best to put colours into her head. He was quite successful, at that. It is since this famous encounter in Pouldreuzic that we have seen the market in white goods swamped by mauve napkins, blue pillowslips, green tablecloths and pink sheets.

When she had hung her linen out in the sun, Columbine went back into the laundry. Harlequin, who was carrying the empty basket, offered to repaint the façade of her house. Columbine accepted. Harlequin went to work at once. He dismantled his caravan and used the bits and pieces to erect a scaffold over the front of the laundry. It was as if the dismantled caravan had taken possession of Columbine's house. Harlequin nimbly jumped up on to his scaffolding. With his multicoloured leotard and his crest of red hair, he looked like an exotic bird on its perch. And as if to stress the resemblance, he sang and whistled with gusto. From time to time Columbine's head came out of the window, and they exchanged jokes, smiles and songs.

Harlequin's work took shape very quickly. The white façade of the house disappeared under a multicoloured palette. There were all the colours of the rainbow plus a few more, but neither black, nor white, nor grey. But above all there were two of Harlequin's inventions that would prove, if necessary, that he was really the most enterprising and most insolent of all house painters. In the first place, he painted a life-sized portrait of Columbine on the wall, in which she was carrying her linen basket on her head. But that wasn't all. Instead of painting this Columbine in her usual white clothes, Harlequin gave her a dress consisting of little multicoloured diamonds, just like his leotard. And there was also something else. True, he had repainted the word LAUNDRY in black letters on a white background, but after it, in letters of every colour, he had added: DYERS! He had worked so fast that everything was finished by the time the sun went down, although the paint was still far from dry.

The sun went down, and Pierrot got up. The little basement window in the bakery began to glow with warm reflected light. An enormous moon was floating like a milk-white balloon in the phosphorescent sky. Soon Pierrot came out of his bakehouse. At first, all he saw was the moon. He felt very happy. He ran towards it, waving his arms in adoration. He smiled at it, and the moon smiled back at him. Actually, they were like brother and sister, with their round faces and their diaphanous clothes. But Pierrot twirled and danced with such verve that he caught his feet in the paint pots littering the ground. He bumped into the scaffolding erected over Columbine's house. The shock roused him from his dream. What was going on? What had happened to the laundry?

Pierrot didn't recognize that motley façade, and especially that Columbine dressed like Harlequin. And that barbarous word coupled with the word laundry: DYERS! Pierrot was no longer dancing, he was flabbergasted. The moon in the sky grimaced in distress. So Columbine has allowed herself to be seduced by Harlequin's colours! So she dresses like him now, and instead of washing and ironing fresh white linen, she's going to soak old clothes in vats full of messy, nauseating, artificial colours.

Pierrot went up to the scaffolding. He touched it with disgust. Above, a window was lit up. Scaffolding is a terrible thing, because it allows people to look through windows on upper floors and see what's going on in the bedrooms! Pierrot climbed up on to one plank, then on to another. He approached the lighted window. He darted a glance through it. What did he see? We shall never know! He leapt back. He had forgotten that he was perched on a scaffold three metres above the ground. He fell. What a tumble! Was he dead? No. He stood up painfully. Limping, he went back into the bakery. He lit a candle. He dipped his big pen in the inkwell. He wrote a letter to Columbine. A letter? No, just a brief message, but he put all the truth he knew into it. He went out again, envelope in hand. Still limping, he hesitated, and looked around for a moment. Then he decided to fasten his message to one of the uprights of the scaffolding. Then he went home. The basement light went out. A big cloud came along and masked the sad face of the moon.

A new day began under a glorious sun. Harlequin and Columbine came dashing out of the laundry-dyers, holding hands. Columbine wasn't wearing her usual white dress. She was in a dress made of little coloured diamonds, diamonds of every colour, but none of them black or white. She was dressed like the Columbine Harlequin had painted on the façade of her house. She had become a Harlequina. How happy they were! They went dancing round the house together. Then Harlequin, still dancing, began to do something strange. He dismantled the scaffolding erected against Columbine's house. And at the same time he reassembled his funny sort of vehicle. The caravan took shape again. Columbine tried it out. Harlequin seemed to take it for granted that they were going to leave. Because the painter was a real nomad. He lived on his scaffolding as a bird lives on a branch. There was no question of his staying on. And anyway, he had nothing more to do in Pouldreuzic, and all the magic of the countryside was beckoning.

Columbine seemed quite willing to leave. She put a little bundle in the caravan. She closed the shutters of her house. There she was, with Harlequin in the caravan. They were on their way. But not yet. Harlequin got out again. He had forgotten something. A notice, which he painted with sweeping gestures, and then hung on the house door:

CLOSED ON ACCOUNT OF HONEYMOON

This time, they could go. Harlequin harnessed himself to the caravan and began to pull it along the road. Soon, the countryside surrounded them and gave them a festive welcome. There were so many flowers and butterflies that it looked as if the scenery had put on a Harlequin costume.

Night fell over the village. Pierrot ventured out of the bakery. Still limping, he went over to Columbine's house. Everything was shut up. Suddenly he saw the notice. It was so hideous, he couldn't even read it. He rubbed his eyes. He had to bow to the evidence, though. So, still hobbling, he went back into his bakehouse. He soon came out again. He too had his notice. He hung it on his door, and then slammed it shut. It read:

CLOSED ON ACCOUNT OF A BROKEN HEART

The days went by. Summer was coming to an end. Harlequin and Columbine were still travelling. But they were not as happy as before. More and more often it was Columbine who pulled the caravan along, while Harlequin rested in it. Then the weather began to break. The first autumn rains pattered down over their heads. Their beautiful motley costumes began to fade. The trees turned red, then lost their leaves. They crossed forests full of dead wood, ploughed fields that were brown and black.

And then one morning – what a sensation! All night long the sky had been full of fluttering snowflakes. When day broke, snow was covering the whole countryside, the road, and even the caravan. It was the great triumph of white, Pierrot's triumph. And as if to crown the baker's revenge, that evening an enormous silvery moon floated above the icy landscape.

Columbine thought more and more frequently about Pouldreuzic, and also about Pierrot, especially when she looked at the moon. One day a little piece of paper found its way into her hand, she didn't know how. She wondered whether the baker had come by recently and left this message. In actual fact, it was the one in which he had put all the truth he knew, and fastened to one of the uprights of the scaffolding, which had become a piece of the caravan. She read:

> Columbine!
> Don't abandon me! Don't let yourself be seduced by Harlequin's artificial, superficial colours! They are toxic, evil-smelling colours, and they chip. But I too have my colours. Only they are real, profound colours.
> Listen carefully to these marvellous secrets:
> My night isn't black, it's blue. And it's a blue that you can breathe.
> My oven isn't black, it's golden. And it's a gold that you can eat.
> The colour I make rejoices the eye, but it's also thick, substantial, it smells good, it's warm, it's nourishing.
> I love you, and I'm waiting for you.
>
> Pierrot

A blue night, a golden oven, real colours that can be breathed and eaten – so that was Pierrot's secret? In this icy landscape that resembled the baker's costume, Columbine pondered and wavered. Harlequin was asleep in the back of the caravan, not giving her a thought. Quite soon she would once again have to put on the harness which bruised her shoulder and chest, and pull the vehicle along the frozen road. Why? If she wanted to go home, what was there to keep her with Harlequin now that his beautiful, sunny colours, which had seduced her, had faded? She jumped out of the vehicle. She gathered up her bundle, and off she went with a light step in the direction of her village.

She walked, and walked, and walked, did little Columbine, whose dress had lost its brilliant colours, although it hadn't become white. She fled through the snow which made a faint frou-frou under her feet and floated around her ears: flight-frou-flight-frou-flight-frou . . . Soon she saw in her mind's eye a whole lot of words beginning with F, ferocious words forming up into a grim army: frost, flint, famished, folly, fantom, frailty. Poor Columbine nearly collapsed, but luckily a whole swarm of words also beginning with F, friendly words, came to her rescue, as if they had been sent by Pierrot: furnace, fumes, fortitude, flower, fire, flour, flame, feast, fairyland . . .

At last she came to the village. It was the middle of the night. Everything was asleep in the snow. White snow? Black snow? No. Because she had come closer to Pierrot, Columbine now had eyes to see: the night is blue, the snow is blue, that's obvious. But it isn't the garish, toxic, Prussian blue that Harlequin had a whole potful of. It's a luminous, living blue of lakes, glaciers and the sky, a blue that smells good, and that Columbine breathed deeply into her lungs.

She came to the fountain, imprisoned in ice, then to the old church, and here were the two little houses facing each other, Columbine's laundry and Pierrot's bakery. The laundry was in darkness and seemingly dead, but there were signs of life in the bakery. The chimney was smoking, and through the bakehouse window a flickering, golden light fell on the snow that lay on the pavement. To be sure, Pierrot had not been lying when he wrote that his oven was not black but golden!

Columbine stopped, bewildered, outside the little window. She felt she would like to crouch down in front of that glowing mouth breathing out warmth and a heady fragrance of bread. She didn't dare, though. But suddenly the door opened, and Pierrot appeared. Was it by chance? Had he sensed his friend's arrival? Or was it simply that he'd seen her feet through the basement window? He held out his arms to her, but just as she was going to throw herself into them he took fright, stepped aside, and led her down into his bakehouse. Columbine felt she was entering a tender refuge. How comforting it was! The oven doors were closed, yet the fire inside was so lively that the heat came oozing out of all sorts of nooks and crannies.

Pierrot, huddled in a corner, drank in this fantastic apparition with wide-open eyes: Columbine in his bakehouse! Columbine, hypnotized by the fire, looked at him out of the corner of her eye and thought that this kind-hearted Pierrot, there in the shadows, with the big white folds of his costume and his lunar face, did indeed look very much like a night bird. He ought to have said something to her, but he couldn't, the words stuck in his throat.

Time went by. Pierrot lowered his eyes on to his kneading trough, where the big round knob of golden dough was resting. Golden-blond and soft, like Columbine . . . While the dough had been dormant in the wooden kneading trough for two hours, the yeast had done its vivifying work. The oven was hot. It would soon be time to put the dough into it. Pierrot looked at Columbine. What was Columbine doing? Exhausted by her long walk, cradled in the gentle heat of the bakehouse, she had fallen asleep on the flour bin in a posture of delightful abandon. There were tears in Pierrot's eyes as he looked at his friend who had come to take refuge with him to escape a dead love and the rigours of the winter.

Harlequin had painted a portrait of Columbine-Harlequina in a motley costume on the laundry wall. Pierrot had an idea. In his own fashion he would sculpt a Columbine-Pierrette in his brioche dough. He went to work. His eyes kept darting from the sleeping girl to the knob lying in the trough. His hands would have liked to caress the sleeper, of course, but to create a Columbine out of dough was almost as good. When he thought his work was complete, he compared it with his living model. Obviously the dough-Columbine was a bit pale. Quick, into the oven!

The fire roared. There were now two Columbines in Pierrot's bakehouse. At this moment a few timid knocks on the door woke up the living Columbine. Who is it? For all answer a voice was suddenly heard, a voice made weak and sad by the night and the cold. But Pierrot and Columbine recognized the voice of Harlequin, the mountebank singer, although he no longer had – far from it! – his triumphant accents of the summer. What was he singing, this shivering Harlequin? He was singing a song which has since become very well-known, but whose words cannot be understood by anyone who doesn't know the story we have just related:

> *Au clair de la lune,*
> *Mon ami Pierrot!*
> *Prête-moi ta plume*
> *Pour écrire un mot.*
> *Ma chandelle est morte,*
> *Je n'ai plus de feu.*
> *Ouvre-moi ta porte,*
> *Pour l'amour de Dieu!*

For, among his paint pots, poor Harlequin had found the message Columbine had left behind, thanks to which Pierrot had persuaded her to come back to him. And so this glib talker was able to measure the power sometimes possessed by people who write, especially when they also own an oven in the wintertime. And he was naïvely asking Pierrot to lend him his pen and his firelight. Did he really believe he had any chance of thus winning Columbine back?

Pierrot felt sorry for his unhappy rival. He opened his door to him. A pitiable, colourless Harlequin dashed over to the oven whose doors were still oozing warmth, colour, and a lovely smell. How comforting it was at Pierrot's!

The baker was transfigured by his triumph. He made great sweeping gestures, amplified by his long, floating sleeves. With a theatrical flourish, he opened both doors of his oven. A wave of golden light, of feminine warmth and of the delicious smell of pastry flooded over the three friends. And then, with a long wooden shovel, Pierrot slid something out of the oven. What was it? *Who* was it, rather! A girl made of golden crust, steaming and crunchy, who resembled Columbine like a sister. She was no longer the flat Columbine-Harlequina, daubed in gaudy artificial colours on the façade of the laundry, she was a Columbine-Pierrette, modelled in brioche dough with all the contours of life, her round cheeks, her high, rounded bust, and her lovely, firm little buttocks.

Columbine took Columbine in her arms, at the risk of burning herself.

'How lovely I am, how good I smell!' she said.

Pierrot and Harlequin watched this extraordinary scene in fascination. Columbine put Columbine down on the table. Gently, greedily, with both hands, she separated Columbine's brioche breasts. She plunged an avid nose, a quivering tongue into the mellow gold of the cleavage. With her mouth full, she said:

'How tasty I am! You too, my darlings, taste her, eat this good Columbine! Eat me!'

And they tasted, they ate the warm Columbine, who melted in their mouths.

They looked at each other. They were happy. They wanted to laugh, but how can you laugh when your cheeks are bulging with brioche?

The Legend of
Bread

Once upon a time, at the very far end of France, where the land finishes, where the Ocean begins, in other words, to be precise, in Finistère, there were two little villages which lived in a state of perpetual rivalry. One was called Plouhinec, the other Pouldreuzic. Their inhabitants never lost an opportunity to confront each other. The people of Plouhinec, for example, played the bagpipes as they were played nowhere else in Brittany. This was sufficient reason for the people of Pouldreuzic to make a point of shunning this instrument and to prefer to play the bombardon, a sort of flageolet which also has similarities with the oboe and the clarinet. And the same applied in every domain; one lot would grow artichokes, the other potatoes, the latter would be force-feeding their geese when the former were fattening their pigs, the women of one village would wear simple coiffes that looked like chimneypots, while those of the other village would work theirs into little lace edifices. This even applied to cider, from which Plouhinec abstained, because Pouldreuzic's cider was famous. You will ask me: what did they drink in Plouhinec, then? Well, they had an original drink there, which was made not with apples but with pears, and so called perry.

Naturally, they didn't eat the same bread in Plouhinec and Pouldreuzic. Plouhinec had made a speciality of a hard bread, all crust, of which seamen would lay in a supply when they went on a long voyage, because it kept indefinitely. This Plouhinec biscuit was in complete contrast to the Pouldreuzic bakers' bread which was all crumb, so soft that it melted in the mouth. To be appreciated, it had to be eaten hot, straight from the oven; it was called brioche.

Things became more complicated on the day when the son of the Pouldreuzic baker fell in love with the daughter of the Plouhinec baker. Their dismayed families did their best to dissuade the young people from this unnatural union, fraught with difficulties of all kinds. It was no good: Gaël wanted Guénaële, and Guénaële wanted Gaël.

Luckily, Plouhinec and Pouldreuzic are not immediate neighbours. If you consult the map of Finistère, you will see that there is another village half-way between the two: this is Plozévet. Now, as Plozévet did not have a bakery in those days, Gaël and Guénaële's parents decided to establish their children there. They would also be married in Plozévet. In this way neither Pouldreuzic nor Plouhinec would feel humiliated. As for the wedding breakfast, there would be artichokes and potatoes, goose and pork, all washed down with cider and perry.

The question of what sort of bread would be on the table was not so easy to solve. At first the parents thought of putting out equal quantities of biscuits and brioches. But the children objected that it was for a marriage, and a marriage of bakers, and that therefore a way must be found to marry biscuits and brioches as well. In short, the new bakery had a duty to create a new kind of bread, Plozévet bread, equally related to the crust-bread of Plouhinec and the crumb-bread of Pouldreuzic. But how was this to be done? How could bread be made that consisted of both crust and crumb?

Two solutions seemed possible. Gaël observed to Guénaële that they could take crabs and lobsters as their model. With these animals, the hard part is on the outside and the soft part on the inside. Guénaële countered with the example of rabbits, cats, fish, and children: with them, the soft part – the flesh – is on the outside; the hard part – the bone – is on the inside. She even remembered two learned words that indicate this difference: lobsters are *crustaceans*, rabbits are *vertebrates*.

So there was a choice between two kinds of hard-soft bread:

crustacean bread, whose crust forms a kind of carapace that envelops the crumb. And vertebrate bread, whose crust is concealed in the thickest part of the crumb.

They set to work, each pursuing his own idea. It soon became apparent that crustacean bread is much easier to bake than vertebrate bread. Indeed, when you put a ball of dough into the oven its surface dries, becomes golden, and hardens. Inside, the dough remains white and soft. But how can you make vertebrate bread? How can you obtain a hard crust inside the crumb?

Gaël triumphed with his crustacean bread, but he was very sorry that his fiancée's efforts had come to nothing. She was not without resource, though, the little baker Guénaële! She realized that it is the heat in the cooking that creates the crust. So vertebrate bread should be cooked inside, and not outside, which is what happens in an oven. And that was how she got the idea of sticking a red-hot iron rod into the dough as if it were a sort of poker. Ah, you should have seen her wielding her poker like a steaming sword! She clenched her teeth and thrust out her chin as she skewered the loaves with her fiery weapon. Gaël, who was watching her, felt cold shivers running down his spine, because he wondered what on earth could be in his fiancée's heart and mind for her to dream up this strange combat and throw herself into it so enthusiastically. And then, would it always be loaves she would stab like that with a red-hot poker?

But what did it matter? She didn't get any results, and it was only crustacean bread that had been perfected when the wedding day arrived, and it was on that day, and in Plozévet, that the bread we know was officially tasted for the first time, bread composed of a golden crust surrounding the soft, smooth mass of the crumb.

Does that mean that vertebrate bread was forgotten for ever? Not at all. On the contrary, in the following years it was to have its illustrious revenge, full of tenderness and poetry. Gaël and Guénaële had a little boy whom they called Anicet, in the hope that this fragrant name would help him to find his place in their trade guild. They were not disappointed, for it was he – when he was five years old – who suggested to his mother the idea that was to give rise to vertebrate bread. All he had to do was eat a brioche with a bar of chocolate at four o'clock. His mother, watching him hold his brioche in one hand and his bar of chocolate in the other, struck herself on the forehead and darted into the bakehouse. She had just realized that the bone, the vertebra, the hard part of vertebrate bread, could be made of a bar of chocolate.

That same evening, the Plozévet bakery displayed in its windows the first *petits pains au chocolat* in history. They soon conquered the world and became the joy of every child.

The Legend of
Music and Dancing

In the beginning God created the heaven and the earth. And darkness was upon the face of the earth and silence filled the heaven. So God created the stars, the luminaries and the planets.

And there was light.

But it was not only light, for the stars, the luminaries and the planets, as they accomplished their parabolas and revolutions in the firmament, emitted sounds. And without cease a kind of celestial concert could be heard, sweet, profound, entrancing: the music of the spheres.

Then God created man. And he made him both male and female, which means to say that at the same time he had a woman's breasts and a boy's sex organ. And God withdrew behind a cloud to see what Adam would do.

And what did Adam do? He cocked an ear and listened to the melodious song descending from heaven. Then he put one foot in front of the other, stretched out his arms, and slowly revolved round his own axis. He revolved, and revolved, and revolved, until he became giddy and collapsed on to the ground, where he remained for a moment in a daze. Finally he shook himself, and called out to his father, crossly:

'Ahoy there, God in heaven!'

God, who had only been waiting for this call, appeared at once.

'My son, what's the matter?'

'The matter is,' said Adam, 'that whenever I hear that music, I have to dance. Now the spheres are numerous, and their music is that of a veritable ballet. But I am alone. When my feet move forward, they know not what they move towards, and when my arms reach out, they know not whom they reach out to.'

'That's true,' said God, 'if man is to dance, it is not good that he should be alone.'

So the Lord God caused a deep sleep to fall upon Adam. Then he divided his body into two halves, the male half and the female half, and out of this being who had become double he created a man and a woman. When these two beings opened their eyes, God said to the one:

'She is your dancing partner.'

And he said to the other:

'He is your dancing partner.'

Then he withdrew behind his cloud to see what they would do. What did Adam and Eve do, then, when they discovered that they were so marvellously different and complementary? They inclined an ear to the music of the spheres.

'Isn't that a *pas de deux* we can hear?' Eve asked.

And they danced the first *pas de deux*.

'Isn't that a minuet?' Adam asked later.

And they danced the first minuet.

'Isn't that a waltz?' Eve asked next.

And they danced the first waltz. Finally, lending an ear, Adam asked:

'Isn't that a quadrille this time?'

'No doubt,' Eve replied, 'it is a quadrille. But for that dance there have to be at least four of you. Let's stop for a moment, then, and think about Cain and Abel.'

And it was thus, for the requirements of the dance, that humanity increased and multiplied.

Now there were many trees in the earthly Paradise, and by their fruits each one imparted a particular branch of knowledge. One revealed mathematics, another chemistry, a third Oriental languages. God said to Adam and Eve:

'Ye may eat the fruits of all the trees and acquire every branch of knowledge. But of the fruit of the tree of music ye shall not eat, for, once you could read music, you would immediately cease hearing the great symphony of the celestial spheres and, believe me, nothing is sadder than the eternal silence of these infinite spaces!'*

Adam and Eve were puzzled. The Serpent said unto them:

'Go on, eat the fruits of the tree of music. Once you can read music, you will be able to make your own music, and it will be the equal of the music of the spheres.'

In the end, they yielded to temptation. Now, no sooner had they bitten into the fruit of the tree of music than their ears became blocked. They ceased hearing the music of the spheres, and a funereal silence descended upon them.

And such was the end of the earthly Paradise. The history of music was beginning. Adam and Eve, and their descendants after them, set about stretching skins over calabashes and guts over bows. They pierced holes in the stalks of reeds, and twisted copper bars to make pitch pipes. This lasted for thousands of years, and then there was Orpheus, and there were Monteverdi, Bach, Mozart, Beethoven. There were Ravel, Debussy, Benjamin Britten and Pierre Boulez.

But from that time on, the heavens remained silent, and no one ever heard the music of the spheres again.

*Which proves that God had read Pascal.

The Legend of
Perfumes

In the first place it must be remembered that, according to the Scriptures, God fashioned Adam out of the sand of the desert and, in order to give him life, he breathed air into his nostrils. In so doing, he destined him to an existence dominated by the olfactory emotions. It must also be agreed that the enterprise was paradoxical. To place an essentially olfactory being all by himself in a desert of sand – is that not to cause his unhappiness? True, many thousands of years later, there would be a popular French singer who would claim that her legionaire had a beautiful smell of hot sand. But all subsequent experiments have proved that this was pure poetic licence, because sand – whether cold or hot – quite clearly has no smell at all.

Now God, floating one day over the dunes of the desert land, surprised Adam in a strange posture. He was running his nose up one of his arms and trying in vain to extend his investigation by plunging it into the hollow of his armpit.

'Oh dear, my son,' said God, 'whatever are you doing?'

'I'm smelling,' Adam replied, 'or rather I'm trying to smell, because my main feeling is that I'm not smelling anything . . .'

And he turned his back on him, shrugging his shoulders sadly.

God considered the matter. If Adam has to have an olfactory life, he thought, it is not good that he should be alone. But that's not all. He must also have a perfumed environment.

So he went to work and created Paradise. Now Paradise was only a flower garden bordered by woods of sandal, campeachy and amaranth. And every one of those flowers released its own vapour, like a censer, as the poet wrote. Also, the soil in Paradise no longer resembled the dry, sterile, odourless sand from which Adam had been formed. It was a thick, heavy, rich compost, and it was from this material that God fashioned Eve.

Eve opened her eyes, saw Adam, breathed in deeply, and held out her arms to him.

'Come to me, *bel ami*!' she said.

Adam went up to her, and breathed in the emanations floating round her big naked body.

'*Jolie Madame*!' he murmured, fascinated.

They took each other by the hand and made their way into a strangely pure atmosphere, still innocent of any human trace, composed simply of flowers, woods, and animal fur.

'Take a deep breath, my darling,' said Eve, 'it's nature before the arrival of man that is welcoming us, the three notes of innocence – of plant, forest, and animal.'

'The fragrance of the fifth day of creation,' Adam specified, 'because we were created on the sixth day.'

And this was how their happy life in Paradise pursued its course, punctuated by perfumes which were all that marked each day's hours and adventures. An adventure when Adam picked up a black-and-gold ball on the beach and gave it to Eve. An exquisite hour when blue night fell over them after the setting of the sun. Another adventure when Eve discovered an admirable serpent coiled up in the grass, its scales resembling so many precious stones. She was stretching out her hand towards this living jewel when the voice of God rang out from high heaven: 'Poison!' said the voice. Adam and Eve recoiled in terror. But the Serpent reared up on its tail and blew them a warm, vibrant, scintillating, enigmatic breath, to tempt them. They fled, but from that time on they knew they had not finished with the Serpent.

Now there were many trees in Paradise, and by their fruits each one imparted a particular branch of knowledge. One revealed mathematics, another chemistry, a third Oriental languages. God said to Adam and Eve:

'Ye may eat the fruits of all the trees and acquire every branch of knowledge. But of the fruit of the tree of perfumes ye shall not eat, for, once you knew the art of perfumery, you would immediately cease freely receiving the perfumes of nature. Nature would no longer send you anything but smells and, believe me, nothing is more dreary than a smell!'

Adam and Eve were puzzled. The Serpent enveloped them in its poisonous wheedling exhalation.

'Eat the fruit of the tree of the knowledge of perfumes,' it said unto them. 'Once you know the art and chemistry of perfumery, you will be able to make your own perfumes, and they will be the equal of the perfumes of Paradise.'

In the end they yielded to temptation. Now, no sooner had they bitten into the fruit of the tree of the knowledge of perfumes than their nostrils closed up in horror and vexation. At a stroke, all the perfumes of Paradise had vanished, and nothing reached them but commonplace smells. Humus, new-mown hay, dead leaves, spaniels' wet coats, the wood that burns and the ash into which it turns, these are certainly, for us poor post-paradise creatures, the musty smells of childhood which touch our hearts. For Adam and Eve, though, they were one single stink, that of their new affliction. But there was worse. Going up to each other, wanting as before to breathe in the other's soul, together they could detect but a single odour, that of their perspiration. For to win one's bread by the sweat of one's brow cannot be done without laborious exhalations. At this point, with one voice, they uttered the most misbegotten, the most sinister, the most indecent word in the whole vocabulary of international jargon: 'What we need,' they said, 'is a deodorant.'

The Serpent's promises may not have been totally misleading, but it took man thousands of years of trial and error and research until, one by one, he rediscovered the great perfumes of Paradise. When God called Moses up to the top of Mount Sinai, it was not only to give him the Tables of the Law. He also dictated to him the recipe of the first perfume in human history (pure myrrh, sweet cinnamon, sweet calamus, cassia, oil olive). There have been endless glosses on the Christian revolution. Its real meaning is to be found in the treasures offered by the Three Wise Men to the Christ Child: gold, frankincense and myrrh. That is, two great perfumes and the metal of their flask – gold – at a time when crystal did not yet exist. As an adult, Jesus showed that he had not forgotten that lesson of his earliest childhood. When Mary Magdalene anointed his head with a priceless ointment, the disciples were indignant at such prodigality. Jesus rebuked them sharply. Was not this homage due to him as of right?

But it was necessary to wait even longer, and in particular for the France of the twentieth century, to witness a veritable explosion of olfactory inventions by a pleiad of perfumers of genius.

It all began in 1912 when Guerlain launched *Heure Bleue*. Anyone who caught a whiff of that iris, heliotrope, jasmine and Bulgarian rose felt transported into the first twilight of the world, when the first stars were scintillating above the first human couple clasped in each other's arms. And everyone wept in his heart for that climate of languorous grace. It was something else again when, in 1921, Chanel created her *Numéro 5*. It was the indication of a date, 5 May (the fifth month of the year). But it was also the fifth day of Creation that it evoked in our ancestral memory, when there were forests, seas, and animals on earth, but still no men. Then in 1927, Lanvin sent a black-and-gold ball rolling under our feet, the very same ball that Adam had picked up on a beach, and which is called *Arpège*. It was necessary to wait still more long years until Balmain with *Jolie Madame*, and Hermès with *Bel Ami*, reinvented the greeting our first parents exchanged when they emerged from their natal sleep and discovered that they were marvellously different and complementary. As for *Poison*, the powerful, tempting odour of the Serpent, it was Christian Dior who was to recompose it.

Thus every great perfume is a door that opens on to our paradisal past. Marcel Proust made famous the taste of the madeleine that restored his childhood to him. Because it has giant wings, perfume gives us back the magic garden in which the first couple loved each other innocently under the tutelary eye of the Great Divine Perfumer.

The Legend of
Painting

Pierre and I were born in the same year, in the same village. We learnt to read and write at the same school. After that, though, our paths began to diverge. Pierre was brilliant at mathematics, adored chemistry, and won all the prizes in physics, but the only subjects that counted for me were literature, poetry and, later, philosophy. When he was twenty, Pierre emigrated, but I remained in the village, in the age-old ancestral house. I saw no more of my childhood friend, but I had news of him from his parents, who were still my neighbours. Pierre was in the USA. He had studied electricity, electronics and computer science. And he was now, I heard, a big shot in a computer firm.

The higher he rose in his profession, the greater the distance between us seemed to become. The stories and fables I was writing were inspired by popular tradition. For them to be properly nourished, I felt, it was essential for me to remain close to the woods and fields of my childhood. The more my craft developed, the more deeply rooted in my native soil I became.

One day Pierre suddenly reappeared. He rang my doorbell and threw himself into my arms. He had hardly changed. In spite of the distance, he had kept up with my work. There was not one of my books that he had not read and reread. And he had a fantastic proposition to put to me. His firm had just developed an international coding system. Any text could be recorded on a minute device from which it could be decoded into any number of different languages. He suggested that I should become the first writer in the world to benefit from this system. If I agreed, my entire work could be computerized, and then read in the 130 countries that currently possess an appropriate terminal. This meant that my books would be as universally known as the Bible and the Koran.

I was delighted with Pierre's project.

'My business is communication,' he said. 'Yours is creation. Communication is only justified by the message it conveys. Without you, I wouldn't exist.'

'Don't be too modest,' I replied. 'Creation can't do without publicity. I don't aspire to fame or fortune, but I do need to be read. What good is a musician who isn't played, or a playwright who isn't performed? Communication gives new life to creation – teeming, unpredictable life, without which it simply remains dormant.'

And as the only way I can express myself properly is through storytelling, I told him one of the parables of the wise dervish Algazel, more correctly called Rhazali or Ghazali. I added a few personal embellishments, a legitimate practice in the oral tradition.

Once upon a time there was a Caliph of Baghdad who wanted to have two walls painted in the great hall of his palace. He sent for two artists, one from the Orient, the other from the Occident. The first was a famous Chinese painter who had never left his native province. The second, a Greek who had visited every nation, and seemed to speak every language. He wasn't only a painter. He was equally versed in astronomy, physics, chemistry, architecture. The Caliph explained his plan to them, and assigned one wall in the great hall to each.

'When you have finished,' he said, 'the court will assemble with great ceremony. It will examine and compare your work, and there will be a rich reward for the painter of the work adjudged the most beautiful.'

Then, turning to the Greek, he asked him how long he would need to complete his fresco. And the Greek replied mysteriously: 'When my Chinese colleague has finished, I shall have finished.' Then the Caliph questioned the Chinese painter, who asked for a period of three months.

'Good,' said the Caliph. 'I shall have the room divided in two by a curtain so that you will not disturb each other, and we will meet again in three months' time.'

The three months went by, and the Caliph summoned the two painters. Turning to the Greek, he asked: 'Have you finished?' And the Greek replied mysteriously: 'If my Chinese colleague has finished, I have finished.' Next the Caliph questioned the Chinese painter, who replied: 'I have finished.'

Two days later the court met and proceeded to the great hall in grand array to judge and compare the two works. It was a magnificent cortège in which nothing could be seen but embroidered robes, plumes of waving feathers, jewels of gold, engraved weapons. Everyone first assembled on the side of the wall painted by the Chinese. A unanimous cry of admiration went up. The fresco represented the garden of everyone's dreams, with trees in blossom and little bean-shaped lakes spanned by graceful footbridges. A vision of Paradise that no one tired of looking at. So great was their delight that some wanted the Chinese to be declared the winner of the contest without so much as a glance at the work of the Greek.

Soon, however, the Caliph ordered that the curtain dividing the room should be drawn aside, and the crowd turned round. And as they turned, an exclamation of amazement escaped them.

What had the Greek done, then? He had painted nothing at all. He had contented himself with covering the entire surface of the wall, from floor to ceiling, with a vast mirror. And naturally this mirror reflected the Chinese painter's garden in its most minute details. But then, you will say, what made this image more beautiful and more stirring than its model? It was the fact that the Chinese painter's garden was deserted and uninhabited, whereas the Greek's garden was alive with a magnificent throng in embroidered robes, plumes of waving feathers, jewels of gold, and engraved weapons. And all these people were moving and gesticulating, and recognized themselves with great delight.

The Greek was unanimously declared the winner of the contest.

The Two Banquets or
The Commemoration

Once upon a time there was a Caliph of Isfahan who had lost his cook. So he ordered his bailiff to set out in search of a new chef worthy to carry out the duties of head of the palace kitchens.

The days went by. The Caliph became impatient and summoned his bailiff.

'Well? Have you found the man we need?'

'My lord, I am in something of a quandary,' replied the bailiff. 'For I have found not one cook but two, both perfectly worthy to assume this high office and I do not know how to choose between them.'

'That is no obstacle,' said the Caliph, 'I will see to it. Next Sunday, one of those two men, chosen by lot, will prepare a feast for the court and myself. On the following Sunday it will be the turn of the other. At the end of the second meal, I myself will nominate the winner of this agreeable competition.'

And this was done. On the first Sunday the cook chosen by lot took charge of the court's luncheon. Everyone waited with the most greedy curiosity to see what was going to be served. Now the subtlety, the originality, the richness and the succulence of the dishes which followed one another on the table exceeded all expectations. The enthusiasm of the guests was such that they urged the Caliph to lose no time in nominating as head of the palace kitchens the creator of this incomparable feast. What need was there of a further experiment? But the Caliph remained adamant. 'Let us wait until Sunday,' he said, 'and give the other competitor his chance.'

A week went by, and the whole court reassembled round the same table to taste the second cook's masterpiece. There was lively impatience, but the delectable memory of the preceding feast created a prejudice against him.

Great was the general surprise when the first dish arrived on the table: it was the same as the first dish of the first banquet. Just as subtle, original, rich and succulent, but identical. There were laughs and murmurs when the second dish also turned out to be a faithful reproduction of the second dish of the first banquet. Next, however, a dismayed silence weighed over the guests when it became apparent that all the following dishes were also the same as those of the previous Sunday. The fact had to be faced: the second cook had imitated his competitor in every detail. Now everyone knew that the Caliph was a tyrant who was quick to take offence, and who did not tolerate mockery from anyone, least of all from a cook, and the whole court, casting furtive glances at him, waited in terror for his wrath to strike the instigator of this miserable farce from one moment to the next. But the Caliph went on eating imperturbably, and exchanged with his neighbours only the rare and trivial remarks that are customary on such occasions. Anyone might have thought that he had not noticed the incredible practical joke of which he was the victim.

Finally, the desserts and sweetmeats were served, they too exactly the same as the desserts and sweetmeats of the first banquet. Then the servants hastened to clear the table.

And now the Caliph ordered the two cooks to be brought in, and when they were before him, he addressed the whole court in these terms:

'And so, my friends, you have been able to appreciate in these two banquets the art and invention of these two cooks here present. It is now incumbent upon us to choose between them in order to decide which of the two is to be invested with the high office of head of the palace kitchens. Now, I think you will all agree with me in recognizing and proclaiming the immense superiority of the *second* cook to the first. For while the meal we enjoyed last Sunday was just as subtle, original, rich and succulent as the one we were served today, it was actually only a princely meal. But the second, because it was the exact repetition of the first, attained a higher dimension. The first banquet was an event, but the second was a commemoration and, if the first was memorable, it was only the second that conferred this memorability on it in retrospect. Similarly, historical deeds of valour only emerge from the impure, uncertain gangue in which they originated, through the memory that perpetuates them in subsequent generations. So, while I appreciate being served princely meals by my friends and when I am on my travels, here in the palace I wish for nothing but sacred meals. Sacred, yes, for the sacred only exists through repetition, and it gains in distinction with every repetition.

'Cooks one and two, I engage you both. You, cook number one, will accompany me when I go hunting and when I go to war. You will introduce new products to my table, exotic dishes, the most surprising inventions of gastronomy. But you, cook number two, will remain here and be ever vigilant to ensure that the ordering of my everyday meals shall be immutable. You shall be the high priest of my kitchens and the guardian of the culinary and manducatory rites that invest a meal with its spiritual dimension.'